HUNT THE
TOFF

JOHN CREASEY

HUNT THE TOFF

WALKER AND COMPANY
New York

First published in 1952. This reprinted edition published in the United States of America in 1969 by Walker and Company, a division of the Walker Publishing Company, Inc.

Library of Congress Catalog Card Number: 69—16135

Printed in the United States of America from type set in Great Britain.

THE LADY BATHES

RICHARD ROLLISON lazed on the smooth rock, with a rolled towel for a pillow, a cigarette dangling from his lips, a book unopened by his side. The sun was pleasantly warm. His long, lean body was tanned a rich brown, for during the past ten days the weather had been kind.

A mile to the west was his hotel, the Country House by the Sea. To the west and the east were the rocky bays and sandy coves of Devon, washed now by gently rippling blue waves. Here was serenity, rest from wild and violent deeds. For the first week he had told himself that he was without a care in the world.

The first thing to disturb his idleness had been the young woman who called herself Marion Lane. She had arrived, alone, on Friday; it was now Monday. The second disturbance had come with the meek little man who called himself Eddie Marvel, and who had arrived a few hours later. On the Friday evening Rollison had overheard a fragment of a conversation. The couple had not let it be known that they were acquainted, yet the fragment had been a quarrel based on some mutual interest. Also, Eddie Marvel had called Marion Liz, and Marion Lane had called Eddie Harry.

Since then, the couple had not met, as far as he knew. He had, however, observed one fact that might be of some significance. Wherever Marion, or Liz, Lane chose to go, Eddie-Harry followed – until that morning.

Then Eddie-Harry had received a telephone call and gone off in his modest car, soon after breakfast. Marion-Liz had gone up to her room; she was now only a hundred yards away from Rollison. Presumably she did not know that he was there. She had selected the smallest of coves, surrounded by sea-washed rocks and carpeted with golden sand – and slipped out of a flowered dress and into a brevity called a swim-suit. Only a churl would have betrayed his presence.

She stood on the edge of the sea; and she was beautiful. Not just easy on the eye, but superb. Perhaps that partly explained why Rollison had not yet noticed that something was missing – and not simply Eddie-Harry.

Quite suddenly, she ran into the sea. She went like a silver-and-cream flash until water splashed about her breast and face, and then plunged forward with the confidence of a good swimmer, and began to use the crawl in a way which would have shamed most men.

Coming back, she would be bound to see Rollison – and there wasn't another spot as warm and pleasant as this, where he could neither see nor be seen. All things considered, he thought it best to move. He stood up and collected his towel, multi-coloured Turkish towelling robe, his book, and cigarettes. The girl continued to swim strongly, going straight out to sea, but carried slightly towards him by the tide.

He stiffened.

He realized that the 'something' was missing.

It was a little buoy, topped by a small red flag, beyond which it was unsafe for the strongest swimmer. There was a strong current beyond and a nasty undertow. Soon Marion-Liz would be at about the spot where it should be.

He put his hands to his mouth to make a megaphone, and shouted 'Oi!'

She swam on.

'Oi, there! Come back!'

The warning cry echoed back to him from the rocks, but she swam fast and smoothly and unaware of danger. Rollison turned and ran along the rocks, which sloped upwards towards the cliffs above, touching a boulder here and there to steady himself. He reached a narrow fissure in the rocks, squeezed between them, climbed up several others, then hauled himself to a ledge from which the daring could dive. He shouted again.

The girl took no notice.

Rollison glanced right and left, hoping there would be a boat in sight; there was none. But he caught a glimpse of a man standing by the side of tall rocks which would have hidden him, had he not peered towards Rollison. The glimpse was sufficient to show Eddie-Harry, whose sandy-coloured hair glistened, then disappeared.

Rollison poised on the ledge, bent his knees, and plunged into the sea. It had looked a vast distance away, and he was in the air for an interminable time; but he cleft the water smoothly. He'd judged the spot well, too, it was deep enough. He surfaced, brushed his dark hair out of his eyes, and began to swim.

He could see her arms and the silver cap; she was going as strongly as ever and drawing nearer to the jutting cliffs which helped to make the danger. He had been sure that he knew exactly where the buoy should be, but in fact he couldn't be sure whether she was within five or fifty yards of the spot. With luck, they'd meet before the current caught them.

He trod water.

She was only ten or fifteen yards away, still swimming strongly. It was easy to guess that she had told herself she would go to the other side of the jutting cliffs, to see the big bay beyond. Unless one was deliberately on the look-out, the chances of seeing anyone else in the water were slim. He felt the pull of the current.

She drew nearer, and Rollison swam so that he could dive beneath her. She went over him, silvery and smooth as a fish. He surfaced a few yards away and he turned on his back. She was turning and looking at him with eyes which caught the blue of the sea.

'Get back!' He pointed to the shore. 'Bad current!'

She might not have heard the words, but took his meaning.

She struck out vigorously, showing no sign of panic. He followed. The pull of the current soon disappeared, until they were swimming in safe water, side by side. Marion-Liz glanced at him – and smiled. Into the smile she put gratitude and admiration, and the two made radiance.

*   *   *

They lay side by side on the golden sand, gasping at first, then gradually breathing more easily. The sun seemed hot. The faint haze of the morning had cleared, the sea was like burnished metal, and the sand was warm to the touch.

The girl spoke first.

'Thank you.'

'I enjoyed it.'

8

'There ought to be a warning notice.'

'Yes, there most certainly ought.'

They fell silent, and she sat up, with a swift, easy movement, and stared out to sea.

'My clothes are over there.'

She pointed.

'Mine are there.'

He pointed.

'Whose do you think are nearest?' she asked.

'Supposing I go and get mine and come and join you,' he suggested. 'You can walk on the sand to yours, I've some climbing to do.'

'It's lucky you were there.'

'We all have to have some luck,' murmured Rollison.

He stood up, and hurried towards natural steps in the rocks. He didn't look round, although he knew that Marion-Liz was watching him.

Well, he'd seen beauties before, and she was here under a false name, or so it seemed. And someone had taken away that buoy and tried to drown her.

Or was he guessing wildly? The buoy might have slipped its anchor. Yet the sea had been calm over the week-end, and he knew that it had been there yesterday. She hadn't been to bathe before, as far as he knew.

He rubbed himself down briskly, lit a cigarette, and walked leisurely down to the spot where the girl was standing, wearing the flowered dress again, the swimsuit wrung out. The hat lay on the sand, by the side of the gaily coloured linen bag, which matched her dress – as did her sandals. He'd noticed before that she dressed simply and with good taste – just as he'd noticed the tumbling, waving mass of her hair.

9

'Hallo,' she said, and smiled.

'Had a nice dip?'

'If you—'

'Oh, please,' said Rollison, 'don't let's bring that up. It must be nearly lunch-time, if I can judge by the usual signs. Coming?'

She didn't answer at once, but looked about her as if she expected to see someone else; probably her shadow. No one was in sight. Rollison stood watching her, not trying to guess what was in her thoughts. He didn't need to guess what was in her eyes – fear, belated but as naked as she had been less than an hour before.

'Is – is there such a hurry?'

'Of course not, my signs often get impatient.'

She forced a laugh, but it wasn't natural, and looked at him with compelling directness. She was going to talk. She was going to tell him about Eddie-Harry, and perhaps much more; she might even tell the truth.

'Let's sit over there,' she said, and moved towards a secluded spot where a little sand covered some rocks and others stood about it, guarding them from sight of any one except at sea; and there were no boats in sight. She led the way and sat down. Her dress spread out over her legs, all he could see were her sandals and the pink-painted toes.

They lit cigarettes.

'It's lovely here,' she said.

'Just right. I mean, everything is.'

He was looking at her profile, and her chief interest seemed to be the sea.

'Everything *isn't*,' she said.

'Oh.'

She stretched out a hand and grasped his arm.

'I feel – dreadful. Please don't laugh, just listen. It's easy to say "forget it", but not so easy to forget that if it weren't for you, I would probably have been drowned. Even then it wouldn't be so bad, but for—'

She broke off.

He hardly knew whether to be sceptical or not, she seemed torn by emotions which compelled sincerity. She looked away from him, and again the blue of sky and sea seemed to pour into her eyes.

She gripped his arm again, swinging round almost passionately.

'I came here to rob you,' she said.

II

LIZ

ROLLISON pushed his scepticism far away, but not out of sight, watched her tense face, and smiled, as if she'd said that she had come here for a quiet holiday.

'Didn't you hear? I came here to *rob* you.'

Rollison's smile broadened.

'Did you, Liz?' he asked.

She started, dropped his arm as if it had suddenly become red hot, and actually gaped.

He chuckled.

'*Liz*,' she breathed. 'You knew.'

'It's a day for shocks, isn't it?'

'How did you know?'

'I heard you talking with Eddie-Harry.'

'Oh,' she said, and coloured. 'When?'

'Friday night.'

'So you heard us quarrelling.'

'Just the tail-end.'

'Did you know why we quarrelled?'

'I was too late for that.'

'You may as well know,' she said. 'Harry really began it. He's always wanted to have a go at you. I think he thought that if he could rob the Toff, it would be the talk of London. But – I'm tired of Harry.'

Rollison didn't speak.

She said, 'I mean, I'm tired of working with him. We had a quarrel in London. I told him I was going to work on my own in future, and the partnership was finished. I had the shock of my life when he arrived a few hours after me.'

'I can imagine,' murmured Rollison.

'I'd found out that you were here – all Harry knew was that you had left London. But he probably guessed what I was up to, followed me, and – well, that's all there is to it.'

'Except that there's no partnership, and Harry's an angry man. I don't blame you so much, but Harry ought to have known better,' said Rollison. 'We've never actually met face to face, but he should have known that the moment I set eyes on Harry Keller I'd know that he was one of London's most successful con-men. I wouldn't have known you from Eve, so you would have got off to a better start. Ever thought of reforming?'

She began to laugh, a little chuckle which grew into deep laughter. At last she groped for her cigarettes, then dabbed at her eyes. Throughout it all, Rollison had leaned against a rock and looked at her.

'Better?' he asked.

'Much!'

'That's good. Hungry?'

'Not yet. So you really knew Harry.'

'The moment I set eyes on him, I knew I'd seen that freckly face and the round and innocent eyes before. When you called him Harry, I placed him. I was at Great Marlborough Street three years ago, when he was sent for trial for a very neat confidence trick indeed. He can't have been out long.'

'A year.'

'They didn't give him a long enough sentence.'

She narrowed her eyes and looked at Rollison through a faint film of smoke. For a while she had been young and natural and, in spite of what they'd said, almost gay. She changed, and seemed to become older, more sophisticated. There was even a change in her voice.

'You must be almost as good as they say you are.'

'Who are they?'

'Oh – everyone.'

'We'll pass that – but how good do they say I am?'

She considered.

'I've never believed them, and nor has Harry, we had that in common. I've refused to believe that any man could do the things you're supposed to have done, and get away with it. You've a tremendous reputation in the East End, too.'

'What's my reputation about?'

'As if you didn't know! The Honourable Richard Rollison, otherwise known as the Toff, England's one great amateur detective, even consulted by Scotland Yard. You're almost a legend among—'

Again she checked herself.

'Everyone?' he asked lazily.

'All – my friends.'

'Pity – nice people don't know me.'

'You're not at all what I expected,' said Marion-Liz. 'You weren't, even at the hotel. I expected you to be a modern Don Juan, and to throw your weight about everywhere, instead—'

'Spare my blushes!' begged Rollison.

'You were just a good-looking, pleasant man.' She hesitated; then: 'Well – now you know, what are you going to do?' Shadows touched her eyes again. 'And

14

please, don't give me any of that stuff about reforming. I know exactly what I'm doing, and I shall go on doing it. I don't need men like Harry Keller any longer. I'm – I'm going places alone.'

Rollison's eyes gleamed.

'I know. The Country House by the Sea, for a good luncheon, and after that, if you're not careful, Holloway, or one of the prisons which isn't so nicely situated.'

He jumped up and held out his hands; she took them and sprang to her feet with little help from him. He didn't let go, but pulled; their lips met, lightly.

'See how I live up to my reputation,' said Rollison.

She didn't answer; she seemed puzzled, and kept looking at him, glancing away whenever he returned her gaze. They walked up a narrow, stony path to grass nibbled short and smooth by rabbits, then through a copse of beech. On the far side of the copse they turned into the well-kept grounds of the hotel.

Marion-Liz went upstairs.

Rollison made discreet inquiries about Eddie-Harry.

Marion-Liz came down again, lightly but perfectly made-up, exactly the right vision to sit at the window-table which had been given to Rollison from the first, and which he hadn't shared before. The other guests, most of them finishing the meal, for Rollison had been right about the time, glanced at them and at each other.

When they were alone but for the waiter, Rollison looked into the fresh gaiety of Marion-Liz's eyes.

'Have you seen Eddie-Harry?'

'No,' she said. 'Don't talk about him.'

'He's flown.'

'What?' cried Marion-Liz.

'He paid his bill, which makes the hotel lucky, and left half an hour before we arrived,' said Rollison. 'You can have a carefree holiday, and teach me how to swim. And things. Unless you think I'd be reforming you.'

She touched his hand.

'Rolly,' she said. 'May I call you Rolly?'

'Provided you keep the O short and not long.'

'Rolly,' she said, 'let's strike a bargain. Pretend that nothing happened this morning, that I didn't make a confession. I can afford to stay until the end of the week, and I think it will be fun, but not if—'

'Not if I'm full of reforming zeal. It's a deal, Liz!'

*　　*　　*

All went according to plan, until Thursday. Rollison's scepticism remained at a distance, but in sight. Occasionally Rollison allowed himself to think about the missing buoy – which was found in one of the inlets on the Wednesday, and apparently mystified no one else – and the watchfulness of Eddie-Harry.

They danced at a nearby roadhouse on the Wednesday evening, it was half-past two before he turned the sleek nose of his Rolls-Bentley into the garage of the hotel. He left a 'Do Not Disturb' notice outside the door, and went to sleep – and woke, when it was bright day, to a loud cry.

He had the trick of waking to complete wakefulness, slid out of bed and reached the window as the cry was repeated.

At the end of the long garden, partly hidden by a yew-hedge of great renown, stood Marion-Liz and a red-headed youth. A big youth. He had a hand on each of Marion-Liz's shoulders, and was shaking her. She cried out again, but made a sound like gug-gug-gug. The redhead shook her more violently and her head went to and fro, she raised her hands as if to fend him off, but couldn't manage it. At last he pushed her away, and she fell against the hedge.

The red-head dusted his hands.

Rollison heard his words clearly.

'Now perhaps that'll shake some sense into you. You're going to do what I tell you.'

Marion-Liz was too breathless to answer.

'So go pack your bags,' said the red-head.

By then a gardener and an elderly woman guest who seldom left the grounds appeared beneath the window. Both were in a hurry. As they reached the yew-hedge Marion-Liz straightened up and the red-head took her arm. They walked towards the hotel, ignoring the couple, who stood and watched them pass. Rollison put on his dressing-gown. He was on the landing when Marion-Liz came up the stairs. She wore a cream-coloured linen dress, simple and sweet; her hair was ruffled.

He blocked the passage.

'One of your friends, Liz?'

'He – oh, *please*.'

She made to push past again. Footsteps sounded on the stairs, soft and light.

'*Please*,' she repeated.

'Obeying orders?' asked Rollison.

She closed her eyes and leaned against the wall, as if she hadn't any strength left. Next moment, a hand clasped Rollison's shoulder, a muscular arm pulled him round, and a pugnacious face, topped by the red hair of the young man, was thrust into his.

'None of your business,' he said. 'Hurry, Marion.'

She went obediently along to her room. The red-head had not released Rollison, but did so when the girl's door closed. He had an attractive, homely face – some would have called him ugly – a milky complexion, a few freckles, and green eyes; fine green eyes. His lips were full.

'Don't get in her way again,' he said. 'You might get hurt.'

Rollison smiled gently and murmured that he was sorry, and held out his hand. The red-head was surprised into taking it. Rollison gripped and twisted. The red-head drew in a hissing breath. He stood with one knee bent and his arm turned upwards and had the sense not to move.

Rollison let him go.

'I am sorry, really. I should hate you to get rough with me. Marion isn't coming with you, she'd much rather rest here. Good morning.'

The red-head's eyes blazed angrily, and he bunched sizeable fists. Rollison prepared for trouble – but didn't need to. The youth dropped his arms, backed a pace, opened his mouth in a wide 'O'. He looked into Rollison's with an expression normally found on a bamboozled child's face.

'Good lord!' breathed the red-head. 'You're Rollison. *The* Rollison. Great Scott! You're just the man to help knock some sense into Marion. This couldn't be better!'

III

REFORMER'S ZEAL

The young man gripped Rollison's hand and shook it vigorously, glanced at an open door and led the way towards it, words bubbling out of him.

'Trust me to put my foot in it. I'll bet nothing like that's happened to Marion for twenty years! Which *is* your room?'

'Next door,' said Rollison.

'You could have told me.'

'You could have let me get a word in edgeways.'

'Oh, lor',' said the red-haired young man with a most attractive grimace. 'I'm always talking too much, it's the Irish blood in me, I suppose. May I go in?' He thrust open Rollison's door and stepped inside, swept his gaze round, and went across to the window. 'Sea view and everything, eh? Nice pub, this. I say, you're up a bit sluggish, aren't you? It's after nine.'

'I was out late last night.'

'You old dogs!' The young man winked and then became earnest, gripping Rollison's arm again. 'I say, you can do me a heck of a favour. You're *just* the man she might listen to. Marion, I mean. I can talk in absolute confidence, can't I? I mean, a man like you wouldn't go talking to the police and all that kind of thing, or let a girl down, would you?'

'Try me,' suggested Rollison, and lit a cigarette.

'Sure. Well, it's like this.' The young man's expression

might have been that of his grandfather. 'I'm in love with Marion Lane. I don't give a damn what she's done in the past, I want to steer her on to the straight and narrow. But she takes some steering! I've argued and reasoned and pleaded, done everything except go down on my knees to her, but it was n.b.g. So I've changed tactics and I'm getting tough.'

'So I've noticed,' said Rollison dryly.

'I say, did you see it? Look here, don't you think the rough tactics might work where everything else has failed?'

'It would be a help if I knew what you were talking about,' said Rollison.

'But hang it, I—'

'And who you are.'

The young man raised his hands and let them fall heavily, gave his attractive grin again, and went to a chair and sat down. At the same moment there was a tap at the door. A chamber-maid, smart and pretty, came in with tea; there were two cups.

'I heard you were up, sir, and I know how you like your morning tea.'

'Gertrude, you're a gem,' said Rollison. 'Magnificent! Do you think I could have breakfast up here, too? In half an hour, say.'

'Of *course*, sir.'

Gertrude beamed and went out.

'They look after you, don't they?' said the young man.

'You were going to tell me who you are and what this is all about.' Rollison started to pour out. 'Like a cup?'

'Well, I don't mind if I do. No sugar. As a matter of fact, I haven't had any breakfast. I didn't find out where Marion was until late last night, and started off at dawn. Drove like stink to get down here, too. She hasn't been up to anything, has she?'

Rollison took him his tea, but didn't answer.

'Thanks. I see what you mean. Well, I'm just an ordinary cove, by the name of Reginald Rowse. Run my own little business and make quite a good thing of it. Family don't like it much, they thought I ought to have gone into the family show – the law. Not on your life! I – great Scott!'

He gaped.

'Now what?'

'Reginald Rowse – Richard Rollison. R.R. We're almost twins!'

'Not quite,' said Rollison solemnly. 'What's your business?'

'Cigarettes and tobacco. I've several London shops, and a few in the provinces. Side lines too, of course. I do very nicely, thank you. The thing is—' He gulped down his tea. 'Oh, heck! I suppose you met Marion down here, just by chance.'

'That's right.'

'What do you think of her?'

'What would most men think of her?'

'That's the trouble,' said Reginald Rowse, with sudden descent to misery. 'She isn't what she seems. Oh, she's lovely to look at, and she's a wonderful disposition. Trouble is, she had a nasty upset a few years ago. Her father. He was mixed up in some jewel swindle, more sinned against than sinning, you know. He was sent to jail for seven years. It kind of put the iron into her soul. She lost her mother years ago, Pop was the only thing she lived for, and – well, she turned sour on society. Some people would say that she turned bad, but I don't believe it. I've warned her a hundred times that she will only land in jail, and she laughs at me. She's no fool, but she thinks she can cock a snook at the law. She'll come unstuck, it's inevitable. Don't you agree?'

'It has happened.'

'Come off it,' said Rowse. 'You know damned well that she's bound to come a cropper. She's playing the fool. That's how I met her. She works with a nasty little tyke with about a dozen names. They tried to swindle me – said they could get me big supplies of cigarettes and tobaccos at a special discount, had a consignment ready and waiting, all I had to do was pay cash on delivery. I may look a mug, but I'm careful. The lorry-load of stuff was junk, of course – the cartons looked all right, but there were dummies inside. I spotted this as soon as they'd unloaded, and chased after them, gave the little tyke a beating, and started to work on Marion. Look here, Rollison, what's on your mind?'

'When you expected to get cheap supplies, did you wonder if the goods were stolen?'

'Oh, that,' said Rowse carelessly. 'It seemed a genuine business at first, they had wholesaler's note-paper and all that sort of thing. I'm not a buyer of stolen stuff.' He brushed the question aside. 'The thing is, Marion. She won't listen to me.'

'How did you find out where she was?'

'She sent a card to a girl-friend. I ran into the girl-friend last night. So here I am. It wouldn't surprise me if the little tyke—'

'What does he call himself?'

'Harry Keller. Sandy-haired, pudge of a face, eyes like a babe's. Looks as if butter wouldn't melt in his mouth. If we could break his hold over Marion, I think she'd go straight. She *must*.' He looked at Rollison earnestly. 'It means everything to me. I've sworn that I'll get her thinking along the right lines if it costs me every penny I have.'

'Marion isn't in a mood to listen to moralizing from me or anyone else,' said Rollison. 'You might shake her into a different frame of mind. It's worth trying.'

Rowse was eager.

'You really think so?'

'Could be, yes. What do you intend doing this morning?'

'I'm taking her back to London.'

'Is she doing any harm here?'

Rowse chuckled.

'You don't know Marion! If it weren't so damned silly or if it were someone else, I'd be tickled to death. She's a wonderful line of talk, and she specializes in elderly widowers or elderly bachelors gay. They think they're doing fine with her, and she walks off, leaving them poorer by a few hundred or even a few thousand. They don't say anything because of looking foolish if anything ever came out. Anyhow, no one's ever had a crack at her yet, but she'll try her 'fluence on the wrong man one of these days, and after that – well, I don't want her to make that mistake. Can't really expect you to help, of course, but if you do get any ideas, I'll be eternally grateful. Well!' He jumped up. 'Better go and see how she's getting on. The shock should be wearing off by now.'

23

He grinned, shook Rollison's hand, and went out; he was humming to himself as he closed the door.

Rollison opened it an inch, poured himself out another cup of tea and sat on the side of the bed, and listened while scepticism came a little nearer; Reginald Rowse was almost too good to be true. Rollison listened to good purpose. The first sound was a sharp exclamation. The second, a decided slap. He smiled faintly and went to the door, opening it another inch.

Reginald Rowse was backing away from the open door of Marion-Liz's room. His hands were covering his face, in self-defence. She struck at him fiercely. The fury of the attack drove him back along the passage.

'For the hundredth time I don't want to see your silly face again,' said Marion-Liz. 'I'm sick and tired of you. I hate the sight of you.'

'Now, Marion—'

Rowse dropped his hands.

She slapped him twice on each cheek. Then she swung round, went into her room, and slammed and locked the door.

Rowse straightened up, a hand fingered his face gingerly. He had turned beetroot red, and his eyes were smeared. He took out a handkerchief and dabbed at them, turned slowly, caught sight of Rollison, and came forward miserably.

'See that?'

'Two people can get rough,' murmured Rollison.

'It's hell. Of course I could have made hay of her, but couldn't bring myself to it. Think I ought to have put her over my knee?'

'She might have resisted,' said Rollison mildly.

'Hang it, what can I *do*?'

'Let her have six months in jail.'

'Damn it, I can't do that,' protested Rowse.

Before Rollison could speak, a man reached the top of the stairs – a heavily built man, dressed in a dark suit which made him look as if he were on business; certainly he wasn't a guest. Behind him came a worried-looking middle-aged man – Proctor, owner of the Country House by the Sea.

'Yes, she's in, Inspector, but I can't imagine what you want with her. She—'

He saw Rollison and Rowse, and stopped abruptly. They passed, on the way to Marion's room. Rowse gripped Rollison's arm very tightly, and spoke when they were out of earshot.

'Did you hear that? *Inspector*. The police are after her. Oh, what a fool she's been!'

IV

QUESTIONS

ROLLISON left his door ajar, so that he would hear when the inspector left Marion's room, and whether he left alone. A door opened and closed and a man's footsteps sounded, but not Marion's. They drew near – and stopped. Rollison finished his tea and stood up as a tap came at the door.

'Come in.'

Chief Inspector Allen, of the local police, had a fresh complexion and a big face, wide-set grey eyes which had an ingenuous look, a silky brown moustache, and a heavy jowl. When he smiled, it was as if he were making a special effort to be amiable, for his natural expression was almost mournful. He carried a Homburg hat, was dressed in a well-cut suit, and he looked warm.

'Good morning,' said Rollison.

'Good morning, sir.'

Allen offered his card.

'Police, eh? What's up?'

'You are Mr. Rollison, sir, aren't you?'

'Yes.'

'*The* Mr. Rollison?'

Rollison chuckled.

'Some might say so.'

'I know, sir – the Toff,' said Allen, who did not even try to smile. 'I just wanted to make sure – you are that Mr. Rollison, aren't you? Of London.'

'Oh, yes.'

'Very glad to make your acquaintance,' said Allen. 'I'd be grateful if you would answer a few questions.'

'Go ahead.'

'Very good of you,' said Allen. 'Where were you last night, Mr. Rollison?'

'What time?'

'Seven o'clock onwards, sir.'

'I was here until eight-thirty, went off just afterwards, drove about for a couple of hours, finished up at Latchet's Roadhouse about eleven, and stayed until two o'clock. Too late, Inspector, that's why I'm not dressed yet.'

'I understand. Were you alone, sir?'

'I was not.'

'Would you mind telling me the name of your companion?'

Rollison drew on his cigarette, regarded Allen with some amusement, yet knew that behind his stolid exterior there was a shrewd, alert mind; no one reached the rank of Chief Inspector without reasonable qualifications. Allen would do everything according to the rule book, but would do it well.

'Not at all. Miss Marion Lane.'

'The young lady in Room Thirty-one.'

'That's right.'

'Were you with her *all* the time, Mr. Rollison – from seven o'clock until you got back here at – what time would that be now?'

'Two-thirty. We came straight back. No, I wasn't with her all the time.'

Allen's eyes lit up.

27

'Thank you, sir. What time were you separated from the young lady?'

'From seven forty-five until half past eight. She was changing. You know what women are!'

The light faded from Allen's eyes.

'Apart from that, were you with her all the time?'

'Except for ten minutes at Latchet's, when she went to do some repairs. No more than ten minutes – she hated to miss a dance.'

'I see, sir. No doubt about any of this, is there?'

Rollison beamed.

'Not the remotest shadow of doubt, Chief Inspector. Now be a friend, and tell me what it's all about?'

'I'm making inquiries, sir,' said Allen, blank-faced. 'About a Mr. Henry Keller, who registered at this hotel under the name of Edward Marvel – perhaps you met him.'

'Casually.'

'When did you last see him, sir?'

'Now let me see,' said Rollison, and pretended to concentrate. 'It would be about half past eleven on Monday morning. I'd been for a swim, and he was having a walk near the sea. I just caught a glimpse of him. When I got back to the hotel, he'd left. What about him?'

'He was murdered last night, sir,' said Allen.

*　　*　　*

Rollison strolled to the edge of the gardens, which led to the top of the cliffs, through a wicket gate and then along the cliffs. The little sandy bays and inlets looked perfect in the sunshine. Two small yachts, white sails moving like patches of snow against the blue, sailed sluggishly across the bay – one of them disappearing beyond the promontory where the current was so dangerous. Below, a few families were gathered on the sands with their children; this was an isolated spot, and only the discerning came here. He turned a corner and the hotel was out of sight.

He stood watching the horizon.

Superimposed upon it, there seemed to be the round, pale, and freckled face of Harry Keller, alias Eddie Marvel – with the sandy-coloured hair and the innocent, baby-blue eyes. Then over that there came another picture – in which the sandy hair was smothered with blood, for Eddie-Harry's head had been battered and his throat cut.

Allen had told Rollison all that he would be likely to find in the evening-papers; nothing more. At Hexley, a small village on the coast thirty-two miles from this spot, Eddie-Harry's body had been found at six-fifteen that morning. He had been seen in the village inn, where he had booked a room, at half past eight on the previous night, and had died about an hour later. That explained Allen's disappointment over Rollison's story, because if the girl had been with him at half past eight, she couldn't have been at Hexley.

He didn't know why the police had suspected that she might know something of the murder. There were many things he didn't know – the police, as represented by the stolid Allen, would keep much to themselves. But he did know one thing; had he been anyone but Richard Rollison, Allen would have doubted his story.

He might still doubt it; might think that Rollison was protecting Marion-Liz, for reasons of his own.

Rollison didn't feel sorry for Eddie-Harry; the man

29

had been a nasty piece of work. It was easy to believe that he had drawn the girl into his racket – if Rowse's story about her were true, then she would have been ripe for that. Was there any reason why Rowse should lie?

He could see none.

Why had Eddie-Harry been murdered?

It didn't matter to Rollison, nothing in the case was of interest; Marion-Liz was a nice girl gone wrong, but she had her eyes wide open. He was not a reformer, there was no reason why he should exert himself for her, offer Reginald Rowse advice, or stir himself out of the laziness which was induced by this lovely spot. London in an August heat-wave would be abominably hot; he had no business to beckon him, he was on holiday. Let it stay that way. Forget—

'Rolly!'

He swung round.

Marion-Liz, fifty yards away, came hurrying. She was carrying a suitcase, wearing a light coat over her linen dress, her lips were parted as if she were out of breath.

'Rolly, will you help me?'

'Now what? Running away?'

'Yes, I can't *stand* that man Rowse. He'll hang about all the time I'm here and make a nuisance of himself. I must go. I slipped out of the back way, and he didn't notice me. If you would help—'

Was she running from Reggie Rowse or from the police? Could she have any reason for wanting to run from the police because of Eddie-Harry's murder?

'How can I help?' Rollison asked.

'Take me to the station. My other case is in the

room, packed. I've left some money in an envelope, to pay the bill – I'm not welshing. Rowse won't know you've my case in the car. I can walk from here to the cross-roads, and you can pick me up there. Will you?'

He could say no.

'It'll take me twenty minutes or more, you needn't hurry,' he said.

'Bless you!' cried Marion-Liz.

He smiled and walked off, moving fast without appearing to hurry. Scepticism came up and walked by his side, but he didn't discuss the situation with it. The girl went on, still burdened by the suitcase. He sauntered towards the hotel, and went in the back way. From the landing window, he saw Rowse walking about the rose-garden, and then moving towards the yew-hedge – where he could see the girl's window.

Marion-Liz's case was ready; an envelope addressed to Proctor was on the dressing-table. He opened it; there were ten pound notes inside. He sealed it again, took the case and went downstairs – and met Proctor coming out of the office.

Proctor's eyes fell on the case.

Rollison smiled.

'Yes, it's Miss Lane's. She's leaving. You'll find everything you want on the dressing-table, and if it's short, call on me. Don't talk about it yet.'

He took his car from the thatched garage and drove through a beech-copse towards the cross-roads. His gaze roamed over the oddments in his dashboard pocket, and he frowned; a knife was missing. It was an all-purpose knife with one stout cutting blade and several tools, too large to carry in his pocket.

Someone had taken a fancy to it.

31

It annoyed him, but he pushed the thought out of his mind, for Marion-Liz stood on the grass verge near the cross-roads, beauty against the green of oak and hawthorn, her eyes bright when he drew up. She sat beside him, as he put the case in the back. She didn't glance right or left, and Rollison didn't appear to; but he saw the man among the trees.

It wasn't Rowse.

It wasn't Inspector Allen, but it was probably a detective, watching the girl.

V

LONDON

Rollison neared the station. A few cottages were grouped about it, but there was hardly a village worthy of the name. He pulled up outside the little booking-office.

'Have you a ticket?'

'Yes. Rolly, thanks. For everything. Don't lecture me.'

'I wouldn't dream of it. Did you know that I'm a prison visitor?'

'They'll never send me to prison.'

'They will, Liz,' he said lazily, 'if you go on as you are.'

'I'd kill myself first,' she said. Then words poured out of her, hastened because a train was rumbling in the distance. An old porter with drooping moustache came up and Rollison motioned him away. 'I expect Rowse told you something about it. I hate the police, the law – people! My father was as good a man as you'd find anywhere, and he's living in hell. *Hell!*' she repeated fiercely. 'When he comes out, I'm going to have a decent home for him, and I'm going to make plenty of money. He'll never be in want. That's all there is to it, you can't stop me, Rowse can't stop me.'

She opened the door and jumped out.

*   *   *

Rollison drove to London. It was worse than he had feared. Heat rose from the pavements and the roofs, sticky, oppressive – threatening thunder that wouldn't come. Londoners drooped, the women in flimsy cotton dresses, a few of the men in sensible linen coats, but most in suits which were much too hot and heavy. A few daringly carried their coats over their arms, but looked as hot as the others. Taxi-drivers were in their shirt-sleeves, commissionaires outside the hotels could hardly have been hotter in Turkish Baths, but kept on their thick uniforms. The parks were crowded with people seeking the air.

All this Rollison saw when, a little after six o'clock, he turned off Piccadilly and drove to Gresham Terrace. His flat was on the top floor of Number 22g. The houses in the terrace were tall, narrow, and grey-faced; they had neither the beauty of the Regency nor the ugliness of the worst Victorian period; they were just houses, approached by two steps and with an area in front of each. He went upstairs slowly. He wore Palm Beach suiting, and could not have been dressed more suitably, but the heat gathered on the staircase and in the passages – it was like walking through steam. He took out his keys as he reached the front door.

His man, Jolly, was away; and would be away for another week. That was at Rollison's insistence, because Jolly had worked with few holidays for far too long. He had gone with some reluctance to spend a month at the sea with relatives whose children called him Uncle.

Jolly, at home, would have had the door open before Rollison reached it; Jolly made the home. Rollison slid the key in and stepped inside. The flat seemed hotter than the landing – all the windows were closed and the blinds drawn. He took off his coat and made a quick tour of the rooms, pulling up the blinds and opening the windows wide; it didn't make the slightest difference.

The flat had been empty for nearly two weeks; there was dust everywhere, a thin film that would have shocked Jolly. But it was perfectly tidy. In the living-room, which he used for a study, Rollison stood contemplating the wall behind the large walnut pedestal desk; and he smiled faintly. On that wall were the trophies of his hunting – and the most precious prize was a hangman's noose, which had hanged a murderer whom he had helped to catch.

Such a noose would hang Eddie-Harry's murderer. Would it?

There were too many unsolved murders, and it was no one's fault. The Yard were overworked and understaffed; while that was so, there would continue to be too many unsolved murders. He didn't know whether the Yard experts had been consulted by the Devon police; if they hadn't, they soon would be, because they could give a lot of information about Harry Keller.

He turned away from the trophy wall, poured himself a drink – as always, Jolly had left whisky and soda on a table, ready for him to help himself if he should come back unexpectedly. Rollison left the door leading into the small hall open; and could see the letter-box.

There was a note in the wire cage beneath the box. Yet his post had been sent on.

He took his drink with him when he went to the door.

It was a square, cream-laid envelope, and his name was scrawled in pencil: *Mr. Rollison – Urgent.* He tore it open. There was no way of telling whether it had been delivered by hand the first day he'd left or a few hours ago.

Inside was a single sheet of folded paper and a scrawled message – in an easy, flowing hand.

Mr. Rollison, I must see you, it's urgent. You'll find me at Benny Low's. You know me. Don't forget the Hexley pub and our Liz, will you. And don't make any mistake, I mean business. H. Keller.

Rollison glanced at the message again, then walked into the living-room and dropped it on to the desk. Until then, there had been logic in most of what had happened; there was none in this. The problem was to find out when it had been delivered? Surely not before Eddie-Harry had gone to Devon, he could have had a word with Rollison there without difficulty; that suggested it had been dropped in after Eddie-Harry had left the hotel and – obviously! – before he had returned to Hexley, a blunt instrument and a knife.

Yet Eddie-Harry had known he was in Devon. Why should he have to come here?

The telephone-bell rang.

That startled Rollison; everyone likely to call knew that he was out of town. The bell kept ringing. The pencilled message stared up at him from the paper, which was smeared as with damp fingers. That was another indication of the time it had been delivered; according to the newspapers, the heat-wave had hit London on Sunday, until then the sun had stayed in the south-west. Yet when this had been written, it had been sticky hot, and Eddie-Harry or the writer hadn't worried about leaving finger-prints.

36

The bell kept ringing.

He strolled across to the telephone, which was on a corner of the desk, and lifted the receiver.

'Rollison here.'

'This is Scotland Yard. Just a moment, Mr. Rollison, please. Superintendent Grice would like a word with you.'

So the Yard hadn't lost much time in discovering that he was back in London.

VI

ACCUSATION

ROLLISON knew Grice well, but could never be sure
what line the Superintendent would take. They were
friends; at times close friends, although at others
relations were somewhat strained. It was true that the
Yard occasionally consulted Rollison; but Marion-Liz
had omitted to add that more often than not he worked
without them, and as often angered the Powers That Be.

He held the line for several seconds, sitting on the
edge of the desk swinging his leg.

Grice said, 'Rolly?'

'Hallo, Bill.'

'When did you get back?'

'Ten minutes ago.'

'Stay there, will you?' said Grice. 'I want a word
with you.'

He rang off.

Rollison put back the receiver, rubbed his chin
thoughtfully, and picked up Eddie-Harry's note again.
If ever there were a case for telling the police everything he knew, this was it.

There was not the remotest reason why he should
play poker with Grice or sell a dummy to the police.
It was all open and above board – and yet the pencilled
note introduced a faintly disturbing element.

His lips quirked as he dropped the note and dialled
Scotland Yard, asked for Grice, and held on.

Grice was still in his office.

'Yes?'

'Bring me a present, Bill, will you?'

'Don't fool, I'm in a hurry.'

'Never more serious. I just want a set of Harry Keller's finger-prints.'

'*What.*'

'You heard,' said Rollison.

He put the receiver down and went out of the room, through the kitchen and into Jolly's bedroom. This had been partitioned off, so that Jolly's sleeping-quarters were little more than a cubicle. Beyond the wooden partition, installed at Jolly's earnest request, was a small laboratory, and even a tiny darkroom, for Jolly was a devoted camera fiend and also loved to dabble in criminology. Here was a microscope, tiny filing cabinets for keeping specimens, magnifying-glasses, a few simple chemicals – a laboratory in miniature, but everything was good. Rollison opened a drawer in a small bench beneath the window, and took out a bottle of grey powder and a camel-hair brush. He went back to the living-room, and brushed grey powder over the prints on the pencilled note.

The prints showed up clearly.

He blew the loose powder away, went back to his drink and lit a cigarette – and the telephone bell rang again.

'Now, Bill,' he said reprovingly, and went across and lifted the receiver.

'Rollison here.'

'Rolly! You're back!' cried Marion-Liz. There was only one voice quite like that.

'And I had a nice journey, too,' said Rollison cheerfully. 'A little company would—'

'Rolly, listen. I'm in terrible trouble, and you are too.'

'I'm often in trouble.'

'But this time it's deadly,' she said, and caught her breath. 'They think you and I killed Harry Keller. I've just been interviewed by the police, they as good as said I was lying about last night, and that means they think you're lying too. Rolly, be careful.'

'Don't worry, Liz.'

'I can't help worrying. Murder is—' She caught her breath. 'They can't prove that I did what I didn't do, can they?'

'They won't seriously try.'

'Listen, Rolly,' she said desperately, 'you mustn't make light of this. They mean business. I could kill myself for having got you into such a mess. If you hadn't helped me and tried to give me a good time, it wouldn't have happened. Tell them – tell them everything.'

'About what?'

'About me. What I told you. I – I don't see any other way out. They probably know about me, anyhow, and probably guess you do, too. I think that little rat Keller must have squealed. But don't get yourself into trouble because of me, I shall be all right.'

'Where are you?'

'Never mind.'

'Liz,' said Rollison, 'I want to know where you are, and I want you to stay there. No more running away. If you do a flit, the police will really have reason to think you're mixed up in this. Understand?'

'They'll *never* catch me,' Marion-Liz said, and rang off.

Rollison put the receiver down, looked at the trophy wall. Small automatic pistols which were deadly, phials of poison securely locked in small cabinets fitted with toughened glass windows, cracksman's tools, ingenious weapons of all kinds – and all used in cases on which he had worked. Murder was not new to him. Above all the other trophies was a top hat with a bullet hole in the crown. He touched his forehead to that – and the front-door bell rang.

It was Grice.

*   *   *

Superintendent William Grice was a tall, well-built, rangy man, with a bony face and square shoulders. He had a sallow complexion, brown eyes, and wore a brown suit; his hair was brown where it wasn't turning grey. His skin had a peculiar clearness, almost transparency, stretching tightly across his nose. There two little white ridges showed at the bridge, as if there weren't enough skin and it had been stretched to make do. His hair was sleek and brushed straight back from his forehead, with a centre parting. On the right side of his face and temple was an ugly scar; Rollison had been with him when he had been gravely wounded in an explosion.

He was a quiet man, by nature, but could be brisk and aggressive.

'Drink, Bill?' asked Rollison.

'No, thanks.' Grice seldom drank alcohol. 'What the devil have you been doing?'

'Having a nice restful holiday.'

'Don't try to pull that one,' said Grice, standing with his back to the trophy wall. 'I wondered why you'd decided to go down to that out-of-the-way spot on your own, I thought there was something behind it. You've got yourself mixed up with a pretty fine bunch.'

'Accidental, Bill.'

Grice raised a hand impatiently.

'Rolly, listen to me. I know you pretty well, and I know you can't keep out of a nice little mystery. I know you do everything you can to help us, but cheerfully lead us up the garden while you're doing it. I usually give you all the rope I can, because I'm fool enough to believe in your goodwill and that kind of nonsense, but there are limits. You told Allen that you were with the girl all Wednesday night. You weren't.'

'But I was, Bill.'

'Nonsense!'

This wasn't like Grice; nothing in the way he was behaving was like Grice. His agitation was only just beneath the surface, and must have a deep-rooted cause. 'I want to know the truth about last night. How long were you with Elizabeth Lane? Did you let her use your car? Just what time was she away from you? The whole truth, and let me have it fast.'

Rollison poured himself another drink.

'Wrong,' he said. 'The statement stands on simple truth.'

'You're crazy! I know she's a beauty. I know she's a nice girl, if you don't probe too far into her family and her own recent history. She's a damned good little actress, too, and just the type to make you lie for her – your damned quixoticism will get you in trouble one of these days. I can even believe that you think she's innocent, and want to help her – but she's as guilty as hell. If you start building up an alibi for Elizabeth Lane

42

you'll be charged as an accessory,' Grice added flatly. 'It's as serious as that.'

Rollison said, 'Well, well, we're getting all worked up. Bill, cool off for a minute and listen to me.' His gaze was steady, there was no smile in his eyes or at his lips. He held Grice's gaze, too, although the Yard man was obviously impatient. 'I left the Country House Hotel at half past eight last night with Elizabeth Lane, who called herself Marion. Except for ten minutes during the dance at Latchet's Roadhouse, we were together until half past two. That's the truth.'

Grice swung round and began to pace the room. He saw the pencilled note, glanced at it but didn't pick it up. 'You're lying,' he said abruptly. 'You must be lying.'

'No, Bill.'

'Then you were there when she killed Keller,' Grice said heavily. 'You see, we *know* she killed Keller at about nine-thirty in the evening. There isn't any doubt. She was seen with him at Hexley, just after he left the inn there and went for a walk. A girl she knows was there on holiday. The girl recognized her dress, saw her from behind, tried to catch her up, and called her. She ignored the call and disappeared, with Keller. They met near the spot where he was found dead this morning. Other things were—'

He broke off, abruptly.

Rollison chuckled.

'Don't tell me too much, Bill.'

'I won't tell you too much. You ought to be satisfied that if I say she killed Keller, there isn't any doubt about it. Either you've got to withdraw your alibi for her, or we'll have to hold you. That's it and all about it. That alibi is proof that you're lying, she couldn't be in two places at once. Now, face up to it. You can't help her. Even if you think you're digging into a juicy case and by helping her will get to the bottom of it, give it up. It's red-hot. I can square it with the Devon people, provided you drop the whole thing.'

'Liz may be a bad lot, but she didn't kill Harry Keller at Hexley last night, or anyone else anywhere else,' Rollison said. 'You've been led up the garden, Bill. Has this girl friend any grievance?'

'None. We had her in mind because of her known association with Keller. Allen did an astute bit of work, the girl friend said her piece before she knew what had happened. And there was a note in the Lane girl's room – a telephone message asking her to go and meet Keller, at Hexley.'

'She didn't go.'

Grice went to the window, looked out, and raised a hand. That little movement had a significance which put alarm into Rollison – real alarm, for the first time. He looked at the note, and wished he'd never asked Grice about a set of Keller's prints. The note would prove an association with Keller. Grice turned round; he had signalled to a man who had been waiting for him in the street, and the signal was to tell the man to come upstairs. Grice was here as a friend; and couldn't do anything much by himself. Directly a sergeant or detective officer joined him, he would become a policeman.

He wanted the man up here, because two were needed to go through the routine of an arrest.

'Why did you ask for Harry's finger-prints?' Grice demanded.

He looked towards the desk and went to it; Rollison felt sick with alarm, but didn't show it.

He could hear footsteps on the stairs, some distance below, as he leaned back as if he hadn't a care.

Grice picked up the note, read it, and barked, 'When did this come?'

'Your guess is as good as mine. Yesterday, probably. If Harry actually wrote it, it came after he left Devon. Either he came to London and slipped that into the letterbox, or someone else did it for him. He knew I was in Devon, so it doesn't add up. I suppose you're sure he's dead.'

'He's dead, all right.'

Grice took a fold of paper from his pocket – a foolscap sheet. The footsteps stopped outside, so the man's instructions had been to wait on the landing until he was called. Rollison went across to the desk and looked at the ten prints daubed on Grice's official foolscap form – prints of Harry Keller. Grice took a magnifying-glass from his pocket to examine those on the envelope.

He didn't speak.

Rollison moved back.

Outwardly he was quite calm, inwardly he was in turmoil. If he stuck to his story, there would be an arrest. He wouldn't be much good to himself or anyone else in jail. The whole set-up lacked reason, but Grice was sure of himself and wasn't going to take half-measures.

Rollison felt suffocated, and it wasn't just because of the heat.

Grice put both sets of prints down.

'They're his, and that makes it pretty clear that you

had dealings with him,' he spoke in a low-pitched grating voice. 'Rolly, listen to me. Elizabeth Lane met Harry Keller last night, about half past nine, and killed him. There was time for you to drive her from the hotel, go to Hexley, and then go to the roadhouse. Allen's checked that. I don't believe you just drove around. I can't believe you would cover up if you knew what she'd done. She either left you at Hexley or you're lying about the drive. She's still loose, because she'll lead us to others. We'll pick her up when we want to, I've a warrant. She's in a big racket, and we've been after the mob for some time. You probably know all about it and think this is a short cut to the leaders. It isn't. If you stand by your story, I've no alternative but to detain you. That will mean a police-court hearing in the morning and an eight-day remand in custody. Get that into your thick head, and tell me the truth.'

Rollison's feeling of suffocation faded completely, because he had decided what to do.

'Sorry, Bill,' he said.

He clenched his fist and smacked an uppercut beneath Grice's chin. Grice's teeth snapped together, his eyes rolled. Rollison grabbed him before he fell and lowered him to the floor.

Grice lay still.

Rollison turned to the hall, and listened; there was no sound. He went to the desk and unlocked the top drawer. He took out a Yale key, glanced at it and slipped it into his pocket. Then he put an automatic and two spare clips of ammunition into another pocket, added a packet of cigarettes, hesitated, and took out a small sheathed knife which was fastened to a piece of blue elastic that looked like a sock suspender. Next he went to the kitchen and unlocked the back door.

He stepped out on to the fire-escape.

Grice hadn't stationed a man in the yard at the back of the houses in Gresham Terrace; hadn't really believed that the man in the street would be necessary. Rollison hurried down the iron steps, his feet clattering. He reached the concrete yard and looked up; there was only the closed kitchen-door. He walked towards the alley, which led to another street.

Inside an hour, there would be a general call out for him.

VII

GRICE

GRICE came round slowly.

His head was heavy and his jaw painful, and at first he did not recall what had happened. He knew he was lying in a crumpled heap, and his right leg was bent beneath him. He straightened it. The knee joint cracked and the sharp sound brought back memory. He stiffened, lying flat on the floor. Incredulity showed in his brown eyes, dazed from the brief unconsciousness.

'The – damned – fool,' he said, *sotto voce*. Yet his voice sounded loud.

It had to be done.

He dialled a telephone number, savagely – WHI 1212. A girl operator answered him.

'Put me through to Mr. Medley – and hurry.'

'Yes, sir.'

The girl recognized his voice.

Medley came on the line, speaking in a slow, un-flurried voice with a slight North Country accent. Nothing harassed Medley, he was as steady and stolid as they came, and a good man at his job. Grice could picture him, big and compact, coat off, sleeves rolled up, sprawling across the desk to get at the telephone.

'That you, Bill?'

'Yes, listen. Rollison—'

Grice paused.

He could say that Rollison had knocked him out, and

that would do two things: make a complete fool of
him, which didn't much matter, and add a charge of
assaulting a policeman. Nothing would get Rollison
out of that. He gulped.

'Well, has he come across?' asked Medley.

'No.' Grice was brusque. 'He fooled me. Slipped
out the back way. Put out a general call, will you?'

Medley gasped, 'For Rollison?'

'He isn't above the law yet,' Grice said sourly.

Medley almost squeaked.

'So he's done it, this time! I always knew – where
are you? His flat?'

'Yes. Don't lose any time.'

Grice put down the receiver. Medley would sit back
and grin to himself; he had never relished Rollison or
his reputation. Then he would burst into a chuckle, and
start the wires humming. Grice looked down at the
receiver glumly. It was the only possible thing to do,
there had never been a chance of avoiding doing it,
yet – he wished it weren't necessary.

He went to the front door, and opened it. A Detective
Sergeant hurried forward from a corner of the landing.

Grice growled, 'Get back to the Yard, Sims. Rollison
slipped out the back way. His car should be outside, I
doubt if he'd use that – haven't heard a car start off,
have you?'

'I – I've *heard* cars.'

'Check it. Then get to the Yard quickly. Ask them
to make sure all his usual haunts are watched, and pay
special attention to these three – ready?'

'Yes, sir!'

'Lady Gloria Hurst's apartment, Bill Ebbutt's
gymnasium, and the Blue Dog, Wapping. Wherever

49

Jolly is staying – there's a note of that in my office, it's somewhere in Bournemouth. All hotels, all the general places. I'll look round here.'

'Right!'

Sims hurried off.

*   *   *

Bill Ebbutt, a massive man running to fat, nearly bald, with one cauliflower ear, a flattened nose, and the general appearance of the old-time bruiser, leaned against a cornerpost at one of the two rings in his East End gymnasium, and breathed through parted lips as he watched two heavyweights grappling with each other like sleek but clumsy bears. Every now and again, he narrowed one eye, as if to try to see better. Suddenly, he stood up, and turned to a diminutive man in a canary yellow sweater, who stood by his side.

' 'Eavyweights?' he sneered. 'Go and bury them.'

He turned to the second ring, where a couple of bantam-weights, neither of them far into their teens, were ripping into each other. He began to smile; he liked a good fighter better than he liked anything in the world. He had been a useful man with his fists, and for years had trained more young hopes than any other man in London.

The gymnasium was a huge corrugated-iron building. All the paraphernalia stood about – parallel bars, skipping ropes, cycles, punch-balls, vaulting-horses; and all were in use. Forty or fifty men of all ages, but most of them young, made use of the gymnasium every night and paid a modest sixpence for admission.

The bantam-weights stopped at a word from a lanky man who acted as unofficial referee.

'Not bad, not bad at all, kids,' said Ebbutt; and from him, that was praise. 'Now go and 'ave a shower an' a rub dahn.'

He nodded and heaved his great bulk towards the tiny office in a corner, away from the door which led to the street. The office, with a high desk and a high stool and one upright chair, looked crowded when he stepped inside. The walls were covered with photographs of young men stripped for the ring and crouching – and of newspaper photographs and cuttings. In a glass case half a dozen silver cups shone bright and new.

A man called, ' 'Ere, Bill!'

That was almost a sacrilege. Ebbutt was a kindly and generous man, but king in his own domain; and he expected and usually received respect. No casual friend called him Bill when the youngsters were about. He glowered towards the door, for he had recognized the hoarse voice of a man who should have known better.

'Bill!' It was a tall, lanky man in a scarlet sweater, who had a newspaper in his hand and came tearing across the gymnasium, pushing several of the lads aside as he came. There was a dazed look in his eyes. ' 'Ere – Bill!'

He reached the door.

'What do you want, *Mister* Skinner?' asked Ebbutt, in his most bull-like voice, which was laden with what he fondly imagined to be withering sarcasm.

The man in the scarlet sweater and grey flannels had a wizened face, and both his ears were of the cauliflower variety. He came in, holding up the *Evening Echo*.

'Look at this,' he breathed.

'I don't want to look at anyfink,' Ebbutt said in a

voice of dangerous calm. 'You oughta know by now—'

'Put a sock in it,' snapped Skinner. 'Look at that! The Torf's wanted.'

Ebbutt, his mouth open to protest again, stopped, gulped, and blinked. In order to read he needed glasses; outside the office and his own home he refused to acknowledge that. So he closed the door, and took a pair of steel-rimmed spectacles from a drawer in the desk, glowered at Skinner, sat on the stool and glanced down at the paper.

Scotland Yard tonight issued a warrant for the arrest of the Hon. Richard Rollison.

'Nar do you berlieve me?' crowed Skinner. 'An' listen, Bill, there's a couple of busies ahtside, wondered 'oo they was arter. Don't need no more tellin', do yer – they think the Torf might come 'ere. Take a tip – turn 'im in if he does, they wouldn't be arter 'im if it wasn't sunnink pretty bad.'

Ebbutt stared at him blankly.

If he had to choose between his love of the ring and his devotion to Rollison, it would be an even struggle; and Rollison would probably win.

*   *   *

Lady Gloria Hurst, a tall, elderly and patrician looking woman, the one relative for whom Rollison had genuine regard – she was his aunt – woke just after seven-thirty next morning, to find the maid who had brought her tea standing by the bedside and goggling down. Lady Gloria did not like being goggled at even by a favourite maid.

'What on earth is the matter with you? Pour out my tea, Bessie, and then draw the curtains.'

'Yes – yes, m'lady, but—'

'Bessie, if you have anything to say, please say it.'

Sleep took the edge off Lady Gloria's voice and the eagle brightness from her grey eyes.

'It – it's Mr. Rollison, m'lady, he—'

'Richard? He's not hurt?'

Lady Gloria, alarmed, stretched out for the morning papers, selected the *Record*, and read the streamer headline on the front page.

WARRANT OUT FOR THE TOFF
DEVON MURDER SENSATION

Beneath this was a photograph of Rollison and another of Marion-Liz, looking at her loveliest.

Lady Gloria felt the cold hand of fear clutch at her heart. The maid actually went forward, as if to help her, but she sat up, thrust the paper aside, and said clearly:

'I always knew the police were fools.'

The fear lurked in her eyes, even when the maid had poured out tea and left.

*   *   *

At half past seven that morning a man emerged from a small hotel near one of Bournemouth's wooded chines, braced himself in the clear morning air, went out of the trim front garden, and walked across a tarred road towards the cliff-top and the beach below. He chose to walk along the cliff-top, overlooking Bournemouth Bay. Old Harry Rock, defending Swanage, rose clearly out of a faint mist; and across the bay to the south-east the white cliffs of the Isle of Wight were gradually emerging. Nearer, the yellow sand which fringed the huge bay, and the pine-clad, sandstone cliffs rising from the promenade merged with graceful beauty. The pier stretched out; small boats were drawn up on the beach.

The man, who was of medium height and had a somewhat doleful face and large, doe-like brown eyes, walked briskly along. He had a scraggy chin and neck, as if he had once been fat and had lost weight recently. His cheeks were criss-crossed with lines, too, and there were myriads of crow's-feet at the corners of his eyes. Yet he walked with a springy step and did not really look old.

He appeared to be enjoying himself, for he sniffed the air occasionally, although he did not smile. He was dressed in a light-grey suit which somehow did not seem right for him – he was a man who habitually dressed in black. One other man was also having a cliff-top walk, and strolled behind the man in grey.

The first was Jolly, Rollison's manservant for nearly twenty years.

When he returned to the hotel, a whistling news-paper-boy cycled towards the front gate with a bunch of newspapers under his arm.

'Care to take 'em in, sir?'

'Yes, I will oblige you,' said Jolly primly.

'Ta.'

The boy thrust the papers into Jolly's grasp. Jolly winced slightly, and the boy went off, still whistling. There were thirty or forty papers in a roll. Jolly did not undo them until he reached the hall. There, another guest was waiting for them, a man who Jolly knew slightly by now.

' 'Morning, Mr. Jolly!'

'Good morning,' said Jolly. 'You are waiting for one of these, no doubt.'

'Can't wait any longer,' the man said. 'I want to know the form at Newmarket.'

Jolly handed him the first paper in the bunch, and then glanced down at the next – a *Daily Sun*. He actually moved back a pace, as if someone had pushed him. Slowly, he raised his hands. His face looked as if he had just read of the end of the world. He did not even look round, or he would have seen the man who had been walking behind him on the cliff-top, strolling up and down the road.

VIII

FRIEND IN NEED

ROLLISON lay back in a large and comfortable arm-chair, his eyes still closed as if in sleep, but his ears alert. He had been wakened by a slight sound in the next room – a creaking, as of bed springs. This was a small flat in the heart of Mayfair, not far from Gresham Terrace, and he had come straight here the previous night, opening the front door with a key. The tenant of the flat had arrived some time after midnight, and gone into the kitchen and made coffee, while Rollison had hidden in a small but tall cupboard in the living-room. There were two rooms and a kitchen, small but modern.

After the tenant had gone to bed, Rollison had helped himself to some of the coffee, eaten some biscuits and a piece of cheese, and settled himself for the night in the easy-chair. He had taken the pre-caution of locking the bedroom door, to make sure that he could not be surprised during the night.

The bed creaked again.

Rollison got up, rubbed his eyes, and went into the little cubicle called, by courtesy, a hall. A newspaper was poking through the letter-box. He pulled it out, taking care not to make a noise, and opened it. It was the *Record*. He read the headline and the story, his lips twisted wryly.

He walked across the carpeted floor to the kitchen,

closed the door, put on a kettle, and made tea. Fifteen minutes after he had wakened up he went to the bedroom door carrying a tea-tray. The bed creaked again, and he thought he heard a sigh, a yawn, or a mutter of exasperation. He turned the key in the lock, and it made a slight noise.

He sensed the abrupt tension in the bedroom.

He tapped, and called, 'Your tea, madam.'

A girl gasped, 'Who's that?'

'The waiter, madam!'

The springs creaked; she was getting out of bed. He backed a pace. If he knew Iris Cartwright as he thought he did, she would pull open the door and brandish a weapon. So he kept at a safe distance. There were odd sounds, as if she were creeping towards the door, and he saw the handle turn. Then she pulled the door open and rushed forward, flinging an ash-tray at him.

He ducked, and hot tea spilled from the spout of the teapot, and stung his little finger.

'Peace!' he cried.

She stood with her arm raised to throw another missile, a girl of medium height, nicely built, wearing a bright-blue dressing-gown. She had fair hair, now in a net and with metal curlers at the sides. Her face was shiny without make-up. She stared at him, eyes and mouth rounded, and gradually lowered her arm. The second missile, a brass paper-weight, dropped heavily to the floor.

'I'm glad that didn't hit me on the head,' said Rollison.

'Richard, you fool!'

'I couldn't agree more. Like a cup of tea?'

'How on earth did you get in?'

'I walked.'

'But I locked—'

'I had a key. Remember?'

'I *bolted* the door.'

He chuckled.

'I was here last night, but didn't think you'd be in a mood for talking. I hid there.'

He pointed behind him with one hand as he balanced the tray on the other, and went in. There was a large single bed of sycamore, fitted furniture, freshness and brightness everywhere. Iris's clothes were neatly folded over a chair, and her dress had been put away. She backed to the bed and sat down heavily; she had nice ankles.

'Back into bed, and you can have luxury. Mind if I sit here and have a cup with you?'

'Richard, what *is* all this? I don't understand you.' She gulped. 'I remember I gave you a key, but that was months ago, when I was so scared. There was that beastly business going on about my people, and you thought I was in danger.'

She swung her legs into the bed, pulled the blanket and sheet over her, and fiddled with the pillows so as to make herself more comfortable. All this, while Rollison poured tea. He handed her a cup, sat back in a small arm-chair, and ran a hand over his stubble.

'You'll have to get me a razor,' he said.

'Richard, what *is* the matter?'

'I'm a villain, overnight. Iris – how's your memory?'

'It's always all right, but—'

'Good! Then you'll remember, after your mother and father were cleared of that ugly suspicion of murder and everything was going swimmingly again, you said that there was nothing in the world you wouldn't do for me.'

She coloured.

'Yes, I remember.'

'I shall soon know whether you meant it,' said Rollison, and tossed the *Record* to her.

She read the headline, stared at him, read the article, and looked at him again – and then she began to sip her tea. She was determinedly counting ten. Iris Cartwright, victim of an impulsive nature, had tried counting ten before committing herself to anything for a long time; and occasionally she succeeded.

'And I suppose you want me to hide you,' she said at last.

'That's right, Iris. For a little while.'

'Why on earth did you come here?'

'There were three reasons. First, I had a key. Second, because I thought you'd turn your nose up at the police, they guessed wrong so often about your parents. And third, because I can't imagine anyone doing what I want you to do half as successfully as you.'

He sipped his tea, then took out cigarettes.

She shook her head.

'I don't smoke before lunch. Richard, do you know anything about this murder?'

'I knew Keller. I also knew Marion—'

She sniffed.

'*That's* obvious.'

He chuckled.

'Anyone bursting in on us now would talk about things being obvious, and how wrong he'd be.'

'That's different,' said Iris. She looked at the newspaper again. 'She's rather nice looking, isn't she?

Anyhow, your private life is nothing to do with me, but – I can't hide you here. Not for long, that is. To-morrow night I've a friend coming to stay. I could put her off, but it would be awfully difficult. Anyhow—'

Iris broke off.

Rollison didn't speak.

Iris said in a husky voice, 'I'm sorry, Richard. Of course I'll put her off, if necessary, and I don't care what people might say. How can I help?'

'Now that really is my Iris,' said Rollison. 'The first thing I need is to get a message to Jolly. He's away at the moment, but he'll be back in London on the first train after he hears the news. After an early lunch, you can telephone my flat – you'll recognize Jolly's voice, won't you?'

'Good heavens, yes!'

'And you'll give him a message which will fool the police, who'll probably be listening in,' said Rollison. 'And after that, you might see if you can get in touch with a certain Mr. Reginald Rowse, who wants to marry Marion. He owns a chain of cigarette shops.'

'Yes,' said Iris, almost eagerly.

'And then you'll go and see my Aunt Gloria, who—'

'You know, Richard, sometimes you just make things difficult for the sake of it. Why should I tell Jolly and ask for trouble with the police? They would be bound to find out. The best thing to do is to go and see your aunt. I can tell her, and she can tell Jolly. Of course, you don't agree, but—'

'Oh, I agree. I'm both humbled and gratified. I chose exactly the right place to come for calm and common sense. Go and see Old Glory, as soon as you can. There may be a policeman outside her flat – if there is, dodge him.'

'Pooh,' said Iris scornfully. 'I'll telephone her and arrange to meet her for coffee or something this morning. Get out! I must get up.'

Rollison got up hastily, collected the tray and her cup and saucer, and went out. He washed up. He was ravenous, but that was momentarily forgotten when he caught a glimpse of his face in the mirror; his stubble was much more black than grey. He washed, wondering if Iris had a spare tooth-brush.

She came rushing into the kitchen, wearing a green dress, with her hair combed out, and make-up on.

'It's nearly half past nine!'

'Well, you can't have coffee much before eleven.'

'There's a lot to do before eleven,' said Iris, 'and *I* want some breakfast. You'll find a razor and some shaving-cream in the bathroom. I keep it because father nearly always forgets his, and a new tooth-brush, the one with the green handle. You can have' – she glanced at the mantelpiece clock – 'exactly twenty minutes.'

Rollison bathed and shaved and was in the kitchen in exactly nineteen minutes. Bacon was under the grill, toast in a rack, eggs frying in bubbling fat. There was just room for a small table in the kitchen, and a green cloth was spread over it, with some knives and forks and crockery in no kind of order.

'If you want to be useful, lay the table,' said Iris. 'I hope you have tea for breakfast.'

Iris spent three minutes of concentrated energy on dishing up, then put a well-filled plate at each end of the table, shook and licked her fingers because the plates were hot, and sat down.

'The condemned man ate a hearty breakfast,' murmured Rollison. 'Don't you ever think of your figure?'

'My figure's all right,' said Iris, truthfully.

She ate with obvious relish, was as natural as if they breakfasted with each other every day of the week. Towards the end of the meal her attention wandered from the food and she kept glancing at the newspaper.

'Richard, are you *really* in danger?'

'It looks rather like it.'

'This isn't bluff or anything, is it? I mean, you haven't made an arrangement with the police so that some crooks *think* you're on the run, have you?'

'No.'

'Did you kill this Keller man, Richard?' she added, 'please don't lie to me. I don't care what you've done, but I do want to *know*. I mean, if you had a fight with this man and he died, it would be self-defence or justifiable homicide or something, wouldn't it?'

'I wasn't within thirty miles of him when he died.'

'Oh.' Her eyes were filled with speculation. 'Richard, during our family trouble, you were always telling me that although the police slipped up sometimes, they were usually right. They know all about you, they've a great respect for you, I could tell that. Surely they wouldn't issue a warrant for your arrest if they weren't pretty sure of themselves.'

'They're sure,' said Rollison.

'I see. What about this girl, Elizabeth-sometimes-known-as-Marion-Lane? Did she do it?'

'That's what all the argument is about. She was with

me at the time, but they think she was somewhere else. I'm defending a maiden's honour.'

'Honour!' exclaimed Iris sceptically. 'I suppose she was one of your flames – oh, that doesn't matter, and if neither of you did it no one can prove you did. But what on earth made you run away?'

'Remind me, some time, that I have to apologize to Grice,' said Rollison.

'What I can't understand is how you'll be able to help yourself, skulking away somewhere like this,' said Iris, with blistering frankness. 'I mean, there isn't much you can do, is there? You'll have all your work cut out to keep away from the police. If you leave here, you'll probably run into them. What is it you want to do?'

'Find the lady.'

'But she's wanted by the police, and may be under arrest by now.'

'They're only watching her.'

'I suppose you know what you're about,' said Iris. 'Great Scott, it's twenty-past ten!' She jumped up. 'I'll telephone your aunt – I don't suppose *her* line will be tapped, will it?'

'Just tell her how upset you are and can you help and you must see her.'

'All right. You can wash up,' said Iris, and hurried from the room.

Rollison heard Iris talking on the telephone, saying nothing that could easily arouse the suspicions of any policeman who might be listening in. There was a practical common sense about Iris. She came in breezily.

'Eleven o'clock, Fortnum and Mason's,' she announced. 'I'll have to fly. If anyone comes, don't answer the door.'

63

'No, ma'am,' murmured Rollison.

'And now tell me what to say to your aunt, please.'

Rollison talked earnestly for ten minutes, and later, from the window, watched her walking along the street. She disappeared round a corner.

A few minutes later Rollison heard a small car snorting along the street, and caught a glimpse of Iris driving a rèd two-seater as if she were nearing the end of a road race.

*　　*　　*

Lady Gloria Hurst looked out of the window of her flat, after Iris had telephoned, and saw a large man strolling up and down. She did not need telling that he was a detective; and his presence did not surprise her. The police would expect Rollison to get in touch with her, with Jolly, or with that remarkable rough diamond, William Ebbutt; and because they meant to catch him, they would have all three closely watched. She even considered the possibility that her telephone line was tapped, but was reassured because Iris had said nothing to suggest that she knew where Rollison was; only that she was desperately worried, and did want to try to help – and said more, between the lines.

The police were quite capable of reading between the lines. If they had been listening, they knew of the appointment at Fortnum and Mason's.

She touched the telephone, to ring for a taxi – and the bell pealed out. She felt a spasm of nervousness.

'Hallo?'

'There's a personal call from Bournemouth for Lady Gloria Hurst. Is Lady Gloria available, please.'

'Yes, speaking.' Personal? Bournemouth?

'Hold on, please. You're through, caller, Lady Gloria is on the line.'

A measured voice came clearly, familiar and warmly welcome.

'Good morning, my lady,' said Jolly. 'I felt that I must speak to you as quickly as I could. I am at Bournemouth Central Station, and shall be in the train in five minutes, reaching Waterloo a little before one, if the train is punctual.'

'That's good news, Jolly.'

'I suppose—' began Jolly, and paused.

'You haven't—' began Lady Gloria, and stopped.

'I have not had any communication from Mr. Rollison for several days, my lady,' said Jolly. 'I read the news in the papers this morning, it was a complete surprise and a severe shock. The one thing obvious, of course, is that the police are gravely wrong.'

'Yes, Jolly, of course.'

'And I shall exert myself in every way to prove that,' said Jolly. 'I feel sure that you will be equally anxious, and wondered if I might make an appointment to see you as soon as I reach London.'

'Go straight to Gresham Terrace and wait there for me,' said Lady Gloria.

'Very good, my lady.'

'And don't sound so down in the mouth,' said Lady Gloria.

When she rang off, she stood quite still, looking at the wall. The shadow of fear remained in her eyes; and she knew that it was in Jolly's. There was dread in both of them – that Rollison had for once made a mistake, had plunged into mystery and been trapped by his own daring.

65

'Nonsense!' Lady Gloria said aloud, and telephoned for a taxi to call for her at twenty minutes to eleven.

* * *

Grice didn't leave his office for lunch that day, but had sandwiches sent up from the canteen, while he ploughed through a mass of papers and memos. Reports that Rollison had been seen during the morning came from all parts of London, all over the Home Counties, as far north as Manchester, and as far south as Devon.

Now and again, Grice touched his chin, gingerly.

At half past one the telephone rang.

'Grice speaking.'

'Sergeant Middleton here, sir, to report.'

'Yes, Middleton.'

Grice was eager.

'I'll repeat some of it, sir, if I may. Lady Gloria went to Fortnum and Mason's at eleven o'clock, and spent an hour there with Miss Iris Cartwright – who is an acquaintance of Rollison's. Lady Gloria left there on foot and reached Gresham Terrace at a quarter to one. She was allowed to enter, without being questioned, sir, and she had her own key.'

'Yes.'

'At twenty past one, Jolly arrived.'

'I knew he'd left Bournemouth,' Grice said.

'He was questioned at the street door, but allowed to go up,' said Middleton. 'As instructed, microphones were installed in all the rooms in Rollison's flat, and wherever they talk, it should be picked up.'

'Good,' said Grice.

'That's all, sir.'

'What about the Cartwright girl?'

'She bought some groceries and provisions at Fortnum and Mason's and went back to her flat. I sent a man to make inquiries, but she hasn't had any visitors as far as we can trace. Shall I have the flat watched?'

'Might be as well,' said Grice, 'although I can't see Rollison putting Miss Cartwright on the spot. Anything else?'

'Nothing you don't know, sir. The Lane girl is still at Kensington. She hasn't had any visitors, but your instructions were to hold off for a bit.'

'Make quite sure she can't get away,' said Grice. 'And tell me as soon as Lady Gloria has left Rollison's flat. Then I'll send for Jolly and have him questioned, while you put on those records and find out what they said.'

'Very good, sir,' said Sergeant Middleton.

IX

THE WISDOM OF JOLLY

JOLLY stepped inside the flat, and Lady Gloria, tall and regal of figure, wearing a wide-brimmed hat and a dark dress and looking cool in spite of it, came forward from the living-room. Jolly was in a black coat and striped trousers and wore a grey cravat.

'Have you heard from him, Jolly?'

Lady Gloria gripped Jolly's hand.

'I'm afraid not, my lady,' said Jolly. 'It is extremely unlikely that he would get in touch with either of us direct.'

He felt the pressure of her fingers, and guessed there was a reason for it – guessed also that her loud question had been intended for the ears of any Yard man who might be waiting on the landing.

She drew him into the living-room.

'Jolly, I—'

'Excuse me, my lady,' said Jolly, primly – and winked.

It was almost a revolution for Jolly to wink at Lady Gloria.

She dropped his hand.

'It is a most distressing affair,' Jolly said with heavy formality. 'Of course the police have made a grotesque mistake, it is not really surprising, but – why did Mr. Rollison run away? I just can't understand it, I can't understand it at all.'

As he spoke, he went to the fireplace and knelt down, examining it closely. Apparently satisfied, and mystifying Lady Gloria, he stood up and walked round the room, examining the walls and the wainscoting and looking beneath each of the pictures – all woodcuts.

Understanding dawned on Lady Gloria.

'Had you any idea that he was working?' she asked.

'None at all. He gave me to understand that he felt a few weeks of complete rest would do him good – after he was wounded in the last affray, he wasn't at all well, m'lady. He wasn't seriously ill, of course, but he certainly needed a change of air. I advised him to visit the Continent, but he said he would prefer the south-west – he is very fond of the Country House Hotel. He insisted that I should also take a holiday, and I have little doubt that he went without any idea of a sensation of this nature.'

Jolly still poked, prodded, and peered.

'Are you sure?'

'It is very difficult to be sure,' said Jolly. 'On the other hand, he *was* feeling off-colour. To my knowledge, he had not made Miss Lane's acquaintance at the time, and although we knew of the man Keller, we've never had any personal dealings with him. I had time this morning to telephone Mr. Linnett, of the *Daily Cry*.'

Jolly stood in front of the desk, looking down, then lay flat on his stomach and peered underneath – and saw nothing. He stood up, dusting his knees.

'Can Linnett help?'

'He was able to give me some information,' said Jolly, and his gaze roamed over the trophy wall. He stiffened, but didn't interrupt the flow of words, although a curious thing happened – he began to speak more softly as he pulled a chair to the wall and stood on it. He was almost whispering, but his words came clearly. 'Linnett is an extremely able reporter, and gave me this information in the strictest confidence. Mr. Rollison claims to have been in this Miss Lane's company from eight-thirty until two-thirty on the night of Wednesday and Thursday. The man Keller was killed some time after eight-thirty, and the nearest the police can get to an accurate estimate of the time is half past nine.'

While he said this, Jolly was moving the top hat with the bullet hole through the crown, and peering up into it; and he had to lean heavily against the wall, so as to do that without disturbing the hat.

'Mr. Rollison has been emphatic that they were nowhere near the village of Hexley, where the body was found, but Miss Lane was seen there. At least, an independent witness has testified to that, and several local people saw a young woman whose description is undoubtedly like Miss Lane's. Also, the young woman was wearing a distinctive dress, of an unusual material and design. Certainly a young woman of Miss Lane's colouring, size, and build, and dressed in a dress believed to be hers, talked to Keller soon after half past eight on Wednesday evening. Linnett suspects that the police have other evidence: an iron spanner bearing Miss Lane's finger-prints, found near the scene of the crime; two or three hairs, believed to be identical with hers; footprints, which coincide with the size and type of shoe she usually wears. The finger-prints themselves would be sufficient to build a strong case, of course.'

While he had said this, gloomily, Jolly had raised the

hat a few inches, and pointed with his free hand. Lady Gloria went closer to the wall, looked up, and saw the small instrument which was fastened to the peg on which the hat rested; she hadn't any doubt what it was. Jolly eased the hat back into position, climbed down, and began to talk in a more normal speaking voice.

'The indications are, of course, that Mr. Rollison thinks there is good reason to defend the girl, and is taking a great risk in lying about being with her all the time. That is obviously what the police think. Knowing Mr. Rollison as we do, that could be so.'

'Would he be such a fool?'

'In a good cause, yes,' said Jolly primly. 'Will you excuse me a moment, my lady?'

She nodded, and stood staring at the hat.

Jolly was back in three minutes, carrying a step-ladder and a small screwdriver. He put the steps into position, lifted the hat off the peg, and examined the tiny battery-recording unit. He loosened two small screws, took them out and pulled the wire free. He didn't speak for a moment, but went across and closed the other doors.

'I think it is quite safe to speak freely now, my lady.'

Lady Gloria laughed.

'Jolly, you're superb!'

'Thank you, my lady.'

'But are you sure there aren't others?'

'I know the type of instrument. It is extremely sensitive, and would pick up every sound in the room. When we've finished our confidential discussion I will reconnect the battery, and we can talk a little more, for Mr. Grice's benefit. There is one really disturbing factor in this, my lady.'

71

'Yes.'

'If Grice will go to these lengths, he is in deadly earnest. I wish I could understand why Mr. Rollison has run away.'

Lady Gloria said, 'I know why. If he hadn't, Grice would have put him on a charge this morning, and he would have been remanded in custody for a week. He thinks he can use that week to help the girl.'

Jolly gave a slow, satisfied, contented smile.

'So you have heard from him.'

'He is at Miss Cartwright's flat. I've seen her. He wants you to find him a furnished flat, one room would do, where he can go after dark. It must be fairly near here – in the centre of London.'

'I can arrange that,' Jolly said.

'Then he wants to find this Elizabeth or Marion Lane.'

Jolly didn't speak.

'He thinks that a Mr. Reginald Rowse might be able to help,' said Lady Gloria. 'Rowse owns a chain of cigarette and tobacco shops in London, and you should be able to trace him. Richard says that he is young and red-headed, and has the temperament that goes with it. Apparently Rowse is devoted to Miss Lane.'

'I see,' said Jolly, softly.

'Use anyone you like to find her, including Ebbutt,' said Lady Gloria. 'And once you've found her, Mr. Rollison wants to go and see her. He thinks she's hiding in London. He also thinks that the police know where she is, and are holding their hand because she might lead them to someone else. It's what Grice called a "big racket", Jolly.'

'I can well believe it!'

'He was with the Lane girl all the time, and she didn't kill Keller. So he wants to find a girl who could have impersonated her, and also to find someone with a good reason for wanting her to be suspected of Keller's murder.'

Jolly smiled again, serenely.

'Obviously knows exactly what is needed. Did he give you any indication of the motive?'

'He doesn't know the motive.'

'I also have some news,' said Jolly, rubbing his hands together. 'Linnett told me that just over two years ago Miss Lane's father was sentenced to seven years' penal servitude for embezzlement, and for complicity in a jewel robbery. He was a solicitor. He had access to confidential documents relating to the hiding-place of a large collection of jewels, *objets d'art*, and priceless miniatures, worth altogether a very large sum. These were stolen. They have not been traced. I recall the affair well, of course. The police are apparently of the opinion that Lane's unknown accomplices and his daughter knew where this cache was. They think that the girl and the others quarrelled. That the daughter has removed the collection, and that there is a fight between the two parties to secure safe possession of them.'

Jolly paused, then went on with great emphasis.

'The police theory implies that whoever is behind this murder will offer to get Miss Lane out of the country, in return for telling him where to find the collection. As a large sum is involved, the police are not surprised that murder has been committed, and another murder might be committed. If that is the proper explanation,' finished Jolly, 'it is easy to

73

understand much of what has happened. The vital
task is to find Miss Lane.'

'But Mr. Rollison thinks the police know where she
is.' Lady Gloria's voice was sharp.

'I think we can safely leave the details to him,' said
Jolly. 'The immediate difficulty lies in the fact that the
police are watching us closely. I was followed to
Bournemouth Station and met at Waterloo. There was
another in the street, presumably watching you, my
lady. That would greatly distress Mr. Rollison, if—'

'Fiddlesticks!' said Lady Gloria. 'It would amuse
him. And do you think I'm wrapped in cotton-wool?
Mr. Rollison's a fool, he always has been a fool, but he
wouldn't be quixotic about this Lane girl unless he had
a good reason. Only one thing worries me, Jolly.'

'And what is that, my lady?'

'I must have been seen talking with Miss Cartwright.
If her flat is also being watched we'll be in the cart.'

'I remember her flat,' said Jolly almost dreamily. 'It
is on the top floor of a house in a terrace, not far from
here. I imagine that if necessary, Mr. Rollison will
escape over the roofs, he probably had that in mind
when he selected the spot.'

Lady Gloria sniffed, and said abruptly, 'There has
always been a risk that he would get himself into
trouble from which he can't escape. I hope this isn't
the time. Be careful, Jolly – be very careful.'

*   *   *

At half past five that afternoon, while Rollison
leaned back in an easy-chair and read more of Mere-
dith's poems than he had done since his schooldays,
musing occasionally on Iris's love of poetry, he heard

74

footsteps approaching the flat; they were hers. She
had been back, for lunch, and gone out again on
another shopping excursion – and, she had said, to
spy out the land. She opened the door and came in
with a whirl, slammed it, and rushed towards him.
She carried several brown-paper parcels, her face
was flushed, and her eyes sparkled. She tossed the
parcels into a chair, stood in front of him, and burst out:

'How on earth you can sit back like that with all this
going on, I just don't know!'

'It's easy. With so many friends—'

'A fat lot of good your friends will be if the police
come here, and there's a man in the street. A *detective*.'
Iris almost hissed the word. 'I'm sure. I saw him in the
other case, a big man with a flat nose and fair hair.
We're being watched. You'll have to leave.'

'Not until after dark.'

'It won't be dark for nearly four hours. As you know,
I told Lady Gloria everything you wanted, but I can't
imagine how Jolly will let you know where to go.
You're asking the impossible, and—'

She broke off.

There were footsteps outside again, this time heavy
and deliberate, the footsteps of a man. Rollinson closed
the door.

Iris's face blanched.

'Richard!'

'Now take it easy.'

He stood up.

'It's that detective, he—'

The front-door bell rang.

Iris put a hand to her forehead and closed her eyes;
and her lips moved, Rollison actually heard three

words. '*Eight – nine – ten.*' She opened eyes that had become like stars and whispered:

'What are we going to do?'

There was a sound at the letter-box, just audible, suggesting that someone was trying to peer through.

X

NEWS

ROLLISON moved to the window and glanced out, keeping close to the side, so that he couldn't be seen from the street. A heavily built man was walking along on the other side, reading a newspaper. Iris stood with one arm raised, as if she wanted to strike Rollison and make him act.

There was no other sound outside.

Rollison went to the hall door.

He stood looking at it, and began to chuckle. Iris stormed towards him without a word, thrust him to one side and stared at the letter-box across the tiny hall.

A newspaper poked through.

'My sweet, alarm for nothing at all, it's just the evening papers.'

Iris caught her breath. Rollison went forward to take the newspapers, and Iris followed him, clutched his arm, and said urgently:

'Don't touch them!'

'Why on earth not?'

'I don't have evening-papers delivered, I always get one while I'm out.'

'Well, well,' murmured Rollison, and pulled the papers through. 'So someone's sent us a present.'

He took them into the living-room, and opened them out; there was a *Star*, *Standard*, and *Evening News*. The Toff was in every headline, and his picture was on each front page.

Something dropped from the *Standard* and hit Rollison's shoe – a Yale door key.

'Look!' cried Iris.

'Not bad,' said Rollison, and his eyes were happy. 'A present from Jolly.'

He opened the *Standard*, and there was a pencilled note, in the margin, written in Jolly's precise hand. Iris peered over his shoulder, pressing against him in her eagerness to read. They read . . .

'Twenty-seven Lumley Street,' said Rollison, 'top floor, a two-room flatlet, rented under the name of Stevens – isn't Jolly wonderful? I'll soon be away from here, Iris, but never out of your debt.'

He read on.

'Hallo! He's not wonderful, he simply works miracles. "There are three possible places where the woman Lane might be found, and the most likely is at 5 Hilton Street, Kensington – most likely, because the police are watching that address from a flat opposite. It is the flat of a close friend of Miss Lane's, on the second floor. I obtained this information from Mr. Rowse, who was most anxious to be helpful, but was somewhat excitable. He had twice been interviewed by the police, but assured me that he had not given them the Hilton Street address." '

'How on earth did he find all this?' asked Iris. 'Let's read on. "In view of the urgency and my own limited capacity, Lady Gloria made arrangements with the private inquiry agency of Kenways, whose report arrived a few minutes ago. Among Miss Lane's associates are several ex-convicts and others whose activities are suspect." '

Rollison learned everything that Linnett had told Jolly.

Iris gave up half-way through, walked away, and dropped into an easy-chair. Rollison finished reading, then took out a penknife and carefully cut out the writing on the margin, folded the piece and put it in his wallet, and screwed up the rest of the paper.

'We'd better burn this.'

'What are you going to do?'

'See Marion-Liz,' said Rollison absently.

'That woman! But the police are watching her, it would be crazy—'

'That's right, I'm crazy,' said Rollison.

She jumped up, gripped his hands, and peered closely into his face.

'Richard, listen to me. That would be walking into a trap. The police probably expect you to get in touch with her, the moment you go, they'll pounce.'

'They don't have to see me go.'

'You can't make yourself invisible.'

'I can do the next best thing,' said Rollison, and returned her grip, then freed his hands and slid an arm round her waist. 'Don't worry, Iris. I started to gamble last night, this is only increasing the stake. And it's a simple issue – proving that Marion-Liz was framed for that murder. If I can't do that I've either got to retract my story or face a murder trial. Sad but true.'

She drew away.

'I'd hate you to be caught. Is there anything else I can do?'

'What about Reginald Rowse?'

'I've managed to find some people who know a Reginald Rowse who owns some tobacco and cigarette shops, but is it any use now? Jolly's been in touch with him.'

'It might help if you make friends with Reginald,' said Rollison. 'But don't overdo it. After I've left—'

'Rolly, you don't seem to understand, you *can't* leave without being seen. They'll stay outside by night, there's a street-lamp quite near. There's no back way and no fire-escape here. You can't get away.'

Rollison said, 'Let me pour you a drink.'

He went to a small corner cabinet, opened it, and revealed bottles and glasses. She just stood and watched him. His eyes held the brightness of daring, his lean body was relaxed. He was like no other man she had ever known; and he even silenced her fears.

'In the roof at Gresham Terrace I've made a hole,' he said lightly, 'and once or twice I've had to get out by it. Where there's a roof, there's a way, old song! You will stay down here, I'll look at the roof.'

'You'll never do it,' said Iris desperately. 'Your only hope is to stay here.'

'Drink up,' said Rollison. 'Here's to your bright eyes, my sweet.'

* * *

It was easy to make a hole in the roof, although it took some time. When he came down, Iris had overcome her fears sufficiently to be preparing a high tea. They had it, companionably, and he relaxed for a while afterwards; until it was time to go.

* * *

The weather favoured him. Clouds blew up, it was sultry hot, and the thunder could hardly be long delayed. But it was pitch dark on the roof of the house in Mayfair. He hauled himself through and groped his way across the sloping slates towards a chimney-stack, crouched there, and looked back at the hole – and at Iris's head, which disappeared. He had made a neat job of the hole, Iris was going to spend the next half-hour trying to repair it; she might do that well enough to avoid notice if the police should search the flat.

After a while, he was able to see a little.

He lowered himself so that his feet were touching the guttering, and lay flat on his stomach, his head near the chimney-stack. Then he edged his way slowly towards the right – and the nearest corner. He didn't need to go far; two or three houses would probably be far enough; he could reach a fire-escape and climb down to safety while the police watched the flat.

He reached the third house, and pulled himself up and then lowered himself again, so that this time he lay sideways to the gutter. He peered over. There was a square yard at the back of each house, and the concrete showed pale. He saw a man standing near the wall, three yards or so along.

He went on, until he was six houses away from Iris's, then went through the nerve-racking sliding down the roof again. The man was now lost in the gloom, but a distant flash of lightning brought a sudden brilliance, and he saw the watcher clearly.

Thunder rumbled in the distance.

Rollison waited for the next flash, and saw the shape of a fire-escape about ten feet below him. He edged himself over as the first spots of rain fell.

The watching policeman's natural instinct would be to glance up to the sky.

Rollison waited for another flash, and as it faded, lowered himself until he was holding on to the guttering, his feet not far from the iron landing; when he dropped he would make a lot of noise. As thunder cracked overhead, he dropped. He kept his balance and flattened against the wall. In the next flash, he saw the watching man standing against another wall, sheltering from the rain. It was coming down harder, splashing against the iron steps, soaking into Rollison's clothes. He reached the yard between flashes. There were walls between the yards, so he was out of sight and out of immediate danger. He turned up the collar of his coat, waited for darkness and thunder, and slipped into another garden. He climbed more walls, until he dropped into a street which ran at right angles to the one in which Iris lived.

The rain teemed down, splashing up from the roadway.

Lumley Street was a quarter of an hour's walk away.

*   *   *

Rollison found the flat was in a terraced house, between Oxford Street and Grosvenor Square. The street door was open, there was a wall-board, with the names and flat numbers of the tenants. Lights showed beneath several doors as he went upstairs. He reached the flat Jolly had rented for him, opened the door, and slipped into a tiny hall – and saw a light shining from a room beyond.

His hand dropped to his pocket and about the butt of his gun.

A chair groaned, someone moved, a shadow appeared – and then a tall, lanky man, lean as a lath, appeared in the doorway. In spite of the heat, he wore a scarlet sweater with a polo collar. His battered face and cauliflower ears were red from the heat. His sparse hair was standing on end where he had been scratching his head. He rubbed his eyes.

'Cor lumme, fought you was never coming,' he said. 'Can't stay 'ere all night. Crikey, look at you! Raining, is it?'

'Skinner,' said Rollison reproachfully, 'you've been asleep.'

'Wot if I 'ave?' demanded Skinner, from Bill Ebbutt's gymnasium. 'Can't burn the candle at bofe ends, can I? Besides, wot else could I do? Strewth, you aren't goin' to start complainin', are you?'

'Never,' said Rollison firmly.

'Don't sound much like it,' grumbled Skinner. 'If you arst me, it's a ruddy big risk I'm takin'. Don't mind tellin' yer, I advised Bill not to 'ave anyfink ter do wiv it. But you know Bill. Said there wasn't anyone else 'e could rely on, so I come.'

'You're a living wonder,' said Rollison.

Skinner gave a choky laugh.

'You just wait,' he said. 'Come in 'ere.'

He flung the door wide open, and pointed.

A table was laid with a cold collation that would have done justice to a royal buffet. A bottle of wine stood with it, glowing ruby red and bearing a renowned label. Beyond the table, hanging on the picture-rail, was a suit of clothes which might have come fresh from the tailors; next to it a raincoat and a trilby hat.

'Seein's believin', ain't it?' asked Skinner. 'Don't thank me, thank Jolly. Now 'e is a proper marvel. Know wot 'e did? Give a pal of 'is a ticket to go to some cleaners where your clothes was being cleaned while you was away. S'fact. They 'ad the mac, too. 'Is

pal give it to Bill, and Bill give it to me. I fixed it all,
arter that – food as well, Jolly said that brand o' wine
was okay – Burgundy. Suit you?'

'The question is, will it suit us, Skinny?'

'*Us*. You inviting me to dinner?'

'That's right. I'll change first, and then we'll eat and
talk. You've plenty more to tell me.'

'Dunno abaht that,' said Skinner lugubriously, but
his eyes were bright. 'It ain't so much. But I've got a
plan and some tools.' He dived a knuckly hand beneath
his jersey and drew out a canvas roll of tools, then dug
into his trousers-pocket and drew out a fold of paper.
'Wiv Jolly's compliments, 'e says. That's a plan o' the
roof of the 'ouse in Hilton Street, and those next door.
The top flat's empty – people 'ave gawn aht. An' Bill's
fixed a ladder, winder-cleaner's, it'll be easy as fallin'
orf a roof.' Skinner raised his hands and drew back,
mouth widening. 'Strike me, easy as falling orf a
roof – nar wot do yer fink o' *that*, Mr. Ar? Talk abaht
a joke—'

He roared with laughter.

'Mind yer, I'm not expectin' yer'll fall, seriously. Don't
get me wrong, Mr. Ar. But it was funny, wasn't it?'

'Skinny, you ought to be on the stage.'

'Funny fing,' said Skinner, immediately solemn
again, 'I was only saying that to the missus, coupla
days ago. The way I tells a story puts 'em in fits, it does.
Well, wot are you waitin' for? I'm hungry. Oh, I
forgot. There's a car for you rahnd the corner in
Billing Street, a Riley – 'ere's the keys.'

*   *   *

Skinner repeated the story of the missing collection,

the police theory, everything that had been written on the newspaper. He added that Jolly had arranged to have someone at Lumley Street by day and night, and a car handy. There was a telephone. Rollison memorized the number.

*   *   *

At half past ten the last vestige of the storm had gone; the stars were out, but there was no moon. The air was much clearer. Rollison kept the raincoat on, with his hat pulled well over his eyes, as he walked from Lumley Street. Five minutes later he sat at the wheel of a Riley.

Danger waited, at Hilton Street and beyond.

He knew much more than he had known in Devon, but still not enough. Those finger-prints on the handle of the spanner explained why Grice was so sure of himself. No framing could have been done more smoothly; on the evidence, Marion-Liz hadn't a chance.

He couldn't blame Grice or anyone for the line they were taking. There was one way to take the weight of suspicion off Marion-Liz – to find out who had killed Keller and who was framing her.

She was more likely to know than anyone else.

He'd studied the plan, knew where to find the ladder, had little doubt that he could get into her flat. The great danger would come if the police decided to raid it at the time he broke in. If he left the roof way of retreat open, he would still have a chance.

He drew up near Hilton Street, parked the car with the side lights on, and walked towards the back of the houses and the window-cleaner's ladder.

He couldn't see the police, but was sure that they were there.

XI

WARM WELCOME

GRICE pushed back his chair from the desk in his office, yawned, looked at his watch, and grimaced. It was half past eleven. He rubbed the bridge of his nose, stood up, and stretched. The windows, overlooking the Embankment and the Thames, were wide open, and a fresh breeze came in, making it almost cold; and welcome. He stood looking out at the twinkling lights reflected on the river, the lights of the traffic passing to and fro, heard the rumble from Whitehall and Parliament Street.

The door opened.

Tall, dark, and thickset, Sergeant Middleton entered briskly.

'Sorry I'm late, sir.'

'That's all right. How's it going?'

'I've been round and checked everywhere myself,' said Middleton, and sat down when Grice waved to a chair. 'Mind if I smoke?' Grice shook his head. 'Thanks. The Cartwright girl's place is in darkness, she's been out for several hours. She spends a lot of time with an arty set in Bloomsbury. Our men went up, back and front, after she'd gone, and made sure there isn't any light on. We've seen a plan of the flats, and there's no room which wouldn't show some light at one window or other, you can take it that the flat's empty.'

Grice nodded.

'Lady Gloria has been to an inquiry agent – she wants to know a lot about the Lane girl's friends. Normal enough, I suppose, and Jolly would put her up to that. Jolly hasn't left the Gresham Terrace flat. Ebbutt's been at the gymnasium all the evening. One of his cronies, Skinner, has been out most of the afternoon and evening, but looked in at the gymnasium at about nine, and went off again. Nothing unusual about that.'

'Do you know where Skinner's been?'

'No.'

'Could have been up to something, but of Ebbutt's bunch he's less fond of Rollison than any of them. That might make Ebbutt use him, they all do what Ebbutt says. Still, it's too vague. What about Hilton Street?'

'No change.'

'You mean the Lane girl hasn't had a caller of any kind?'

'That's right,' said Middleton. 'This flat belongs to a friend who's away – she let herself in with a key, obviously, and hasn't stirred. As far as the neighbours know, the place is empty. The people in the top flat are out at the moment. If she uses lights at night, she makes sure they can't be seen from the outside. There's a room there where the light could be blocked. She certainly went in, and as certainly she hasn't come out.'

Grice said, 'You're not happy about that, are you?'

'I can't say I am.' Middleton leaned forward for an ash-tray. 'We've had tabs on that young woman for some time. I've questioned several of the people who've strung along with her – the Keller type and some better

87

class. Two or three of them say the same thing – that she always swore she'd never be caught by us, she'd rather kill herself.'

Grice didn't speak.

Middleton stirred restlessly.

'It may have been idle talk, and probably was, but she's been in that place for over a day, now, and hasn't shown her nose. She might have realized that she hasn't a chance of getting away. I don't think she could have seen our men watching, they're well concealed, but she knows that we're on to her. I shouldn't like to force my way in there and find her dead. Wouldn't do us any good. Wouldn't do anyone any good.'

Grice didn't speak.

Middleton said, 'What's the balance, Chief?'

'I don't know. I can't see her killing herself if she thinks she's fooled us. I still think someone will go and see her, and I'd like to pick them up. I shouldn't be surprised if Rollison gets there. So we stand to pick him up, as well as the other people behind this show. It's worth a risk.'

'Even if she kills herself?'

Grice said, 'How serious did she seem?'

'You've seen the reports,' said Middleton. 'She's always done what she said she would do. She started to go wrong after her father was jugged, as far as we can find out. She's boasted that she'll make fools of us, and that we'll never catch her. As far as I can judge, she and Keller got away with quite a lot – we picked up some interesting stuff at his flat, remember.'

'Nothing which incriminated her.'

'She was known to be working with Keller, and he was known to use a good-looking woman,' said Middleton, almost impatiently. 'She's hard as nails and has plenty of guts.'

Grice drummed his fingers on the desk. Middleton lit another cigarette. Except for the sounds outside, there was quiet – and nothing stirred in the office. Grice stood up abruptly, and walked to the window, stood looking out. Middleton scratched his head.

Grice turned round abruptly.

'Double the watch there tonight. We'll give her until the morning, and if nothing's happened by then, we'll pull her in. I don't think she'll do away with herself until she knows she hasn't a ghost of a chance. While she's hiding there, she probably feels that she's putting one across us and having a nice laugh. If anyone goes near the place, hold them for questioning.'

'Right.'

Middleton stood up.

Grice said, 'I wish to blazes I knew where Rollison is. He's getting under my skin.'

'I think I know the feeling,' said Middleton. 'It's hard to believe that he would burn his fingers for the sake of it. Putting himself in a jam like this doesn't add up, but – don't forget those finger-prints. If he was with the Lane girl all that time, then he was with her when she killed Keller. We can't get away from that.'

'I suppose not.'

'Sorry, Chief, but it's certain,' said Middleton. 'I don't get it, any more than you do, but there it is. Even if he retracted now, he'd be in a jam, and we'd have to hold him. There's one thing—'

He broke off.

Grice sat down, rubbed his nose again, and looked up

89

into the sergeant's sombre face. 'Well, what is it?' Grice asked.

'I've been looking up some of the Toff's cases,' said Middleton, 'and one thing sticks out a mile. Every now and again he falls for some woman. It's happened three or four times. Whenever that happens, he goes farther than he normally would. I've also been checking on the Lane girl. She has practically everything. You know Rollison. He's quite capable of taking the rap for this job, while the girl gets away. It's the kind of crazy thing he'd do, if he really thought anything of her. And remember they spent quite a bit of time together at the hotel. I know all about holiday friendships, but is Rollison a man who'd spend all that time with her if he wasn't interested?'

Grice said softly, 'No, probably not.'

'That's what I think's happening,' said Middleton. 'And if it's right, he'll certainly try to get her out of the flat.'

'Yes. Don't forget to double the watch tonight.'

Middleton grinned.

'I fixed that before I came in,' he said.

*   *   *

Rollison crouched on the roof of the house in Hilton Street, and peered down into the street itself. There were two men farther along, undoubtedly Grice's men; and there were two at the back. That could mean that Grice was contemplating a raid; could also mean that he had reason to think there would be an attempt to break into the house that night.

Rollison had reached this spot without difficulty, there were wide sills at the windows. He'd walked over the roofs of a dozen houses. A small skylight led down into the loft; he had to get into the flat below, out of that, and into the girl's.

It was nearly half past eleven.

The skylight wasn't fastened, it was easy to lift it up. He shone a torch inside, and the beam showed cobwebs, oddments of furniture, thick dust, and a water-cistern which gurgled faintly. It was low-roofed. He climbed over, and lowered himself and, when he was at arm's length, his toes touched the boarded floor.

He stood in the middle of the loft, shining the torch.

The greatest obstacle might be the loft-hatch. He kept the torch on as he went towards it. It opened upwards, he could tell that from the position of the hinges. There might be a bolt below.

He opened the catch and pulled.

The hatch didn't move.

He sat back on his haunches, placed the torch so that it shone on the hinges, took out a screwdriver and began to work on the screws. He had all but two out, and those two loosened, before he stopped. Then he took a long, flexible hacksaw blade from the little bag of tools and worked it beneath the edge of the hatch, so that it would take the strain. Holding that with one hand, he took the remaining screws out with the other, then gently prised the cover up until he could get his nails into the side.

He pulled.

It slipped, and fell into position with a dull thud. He listened intently, but there was no sound.

The second time, he lifted the hatch and levered it up until the hasp of the bolt was torn out of the ceiling of the room below – and fell with a clatter. There was silence afterwards. He lifted the hatch back and put it aside.

There was no light on below. He was over the bathroom, and his torch light shone on the white porcelain bath and on a hand-basin. He lowered himself quickly, and found himself looking at his reflection in a full-length mirror. He was covered with dust and cobwebs. He brushed himself down, slipped the tools into his pocket, and placed a bathroom stool beneath the hatch. If he had to come back in a hurry he would find that useful.

The whole flat was in darkness, and he reached the front door without trouble.

He opened it.

Marion-Liz was in the flat below. It was approached by the same staircase as this, and the police might have stationed a man on the landing.

There was no light, anywhere.

He didn't use his torch, but crept forward, groping with feet and hands until he reached the top of the stairs. He went down one at a time, a hand on the banisters. He could soon find the girl's door, even in the darkness he should have little difficulty.

He reached the next landing.

There was only a Yale lock between him and the girl's flat. He listened intently and heard no sound of breathing, nothing to indicate that anyone was watching below. He didn't use his torch, just felt for the lock, then took out a strip of mica and gradually forced it between the lock and the door. When the barrel of the lock was in the middle of the strip, it would be forced back.

He heard it click.

He opened the door and stepped into the flat where Marion-Liz was staying. He closed the door softly behind him; the lock didn't fit properly, forcing it that way had damaged it. He knew the trick of fastening the catch so that it would look all right from the outside.

The bright beam of his torch pierced the darkness like a sword.

A man said, 'Drop that torch. Put up your hands.'

The sword of light showed a gun in the man's hand.

XII

DARK DUET

THE light remained still, pitched on the hand and the gun. The hand was large, with long, thin fingers, browned and powerful. The automatic pistol was fitted with a long rubber snout; a silencer. That kept as steady as Rollison's torch.

Rollison slid his left hand towards his pocket and touched his gun, but didn't take it out. He had no silencer, and a shot would bring the police.

'I said, drop it.'

There was an edge to a deep voice.

Rollison murmured, 'Delighted, old friend,' and dropped the torch, thrusting his foot beneath it to lessen the noise, then kicked it away. It rolled over and over, the light snaking out, now on a polished brown shoe, now the leg of a chair, now on the wall. It stopped. Rollison took two long sideways steps and peered into the darkness; pitch darkness, there was no crack of light.

He could hear the man breathing.

'Don't tell me you can see in the dark,' he murmured, and stepped to one side again.

Flame flashed, vivid and revealing, a bullet hissed out and thudded into the wall. It sounded very close. Rollison stood motionless.

'You haven't a chance,' the man said. 'Not this way. I can give you one.'

Rollison said, 'I like to make my own,' and swift as a cat, moved the other side.

The second shot hissed, and the revealing flame showed a tall man in an open doorway, dressed in dark clothes; only his face and hands showed. The bullet smacked into the wall, as if nothing else was enough to show earnest. Rollison's heart was hammering, and he could hear the other's laboured breathing.

The man said softly, 'You're asking for trouble.'

'I've company,' Rollison said, and stood his ground. There wasn't a third shot. 'Police are back and front, if you keep up the Bisley practice you'll have more visitors. They won't be as willing as I am to keep this off the record.'

The man didn't answer. There was a rustle of sound in the darkness. Rollison took out the gun and held it by the barrel, as a club. The rustle came again, he tried to judge whether the other was in front or to the left or right – and then a white light stabbed out, swivelled round, and shone on his face. He closed his eyes against the blinding dazzle, moved swiftly, felt the glow pressing against his eyelids, following him wherever he went.

He stopped; and smiled.

'Should we know each other?'

'So you've made it,' the other said, and couldn't keep the ring of satisfaction out of his voice. 'The great Toff's come to see me!'

The light was stabbing at Rollison's face, on to his big, glistening teeth.

'Wrong. I came to see Marion-Liz.'

'You can see her, Rollison.'

The shaft of light moved, shone on Rollison's

95

gunhand and the gun. The man drew in a sharp
breath.

'Wondering why I haven't used it?' asked Rollison.
'I should hate to kill first and try to talk afterwards,
corpses are stubborn about talking. Shall we have some
more light and a little chat?'

'Just keep still.'

'I can't do any better than this,' said Rollison, 'I'm
imitating the Rock of Gibraltar quite nicely.'

The man said, 'Drop that gun.'

'Not in a thousand years.' Rollison had a laugh in
his voice – and let it fade, caught his breath and
muttered, 'Listen!'

That wasn't bluff, there were footsteps outside. A
man came up the stairs – perhaps a man and woman.
The sounds stopped. The unseen man's breathing was
harsh and laboured again. Rollison held his breath –
heard a faint sound, as a key turned in a lock, then a
mutter of voices. After a pause, a door closed.

'The old folk next door,' murmured Rollison. 'The
police might follow, to see what they're up to. I
shouldn't start playing the accordion.'

The torch went out; another rustle of movement
told him that the other was moving. Right, left, or
forward? Using his wits, he could guess why the man
wanted to talk: a proposition was on the wing. Yet
there was nothing here to make him feel free from
danger. The thudding of those bullets in the wall had
been unpleasantly close.

'Do you like playing around in the dark?' he asked,
and the laugh was back in his voice.

'Listen, Rollison, I can fix you. It's all laid on. I
can find a witness to say you were with Lizzie Lane

when she killed Keller. That would send you for the long drop. Don't make any mistakes.'

'No more than I can help,' said Rollison brightly. 'But what makes you think the police will think that I stood by while the girl friend battered poor Keller and cut his throat?'

'They'll believe it, if they have a witness. You're in a bad spot already.'

Give the police that threatened 'evidence' and they would have a case so strong that nothing would be able to break it. 'When are we going to have some light?'

His hand groped for the light switch, and touched it.

'Don't do that!' The torchlight shone out again, and stabbed against Rollison's face. 'Back into the room.' The light shone steadily and close to the man's body, for the glow just showed his gun. 'Play the fool, and I'll shoot.'

Rollison backed into the room.

He came up against a table.

The torch went out. After a pause, the door closed, and the man put down the switch.

This was a small room, without a window; a room that had been partitioned off from a large one. He was leaning against a dining-table. There were four upright chairs, a small sideboard, a tall corner cupboard, a few books in open shelves near an electric fire. The floor was carpeted in deep red. The furniture was modern, of fair quality; the walls were papered cream, and the lighting came from three lamps set in the walls.

The door and the woodwork were painted red.

The man stood against the closed door, tall, lean, dressed in navy blue. He was middle-aged; his grizzled hair was thick and heavily greased, brushed straight back from his forehead without a parting. His face was round, his cheeks tanned to a healthy, attractive brown; he had light-grey eyes, and his tan made them seem very bright. He had a short nose and short upper lip, and his lips were full, almost too full, hinting at mixed blood.

'Go and sit on the other side of the table.'

Rollison shrugged, moved, and sat.

'Put your gun away.'

'That's where I stick,' said Rollison. 'If I have to choose between a trial and a shot from your gun, I'll have the trial. Of course, you put your gun away, and then we'd be on equal terms.'

The man put his gun into his coat pocket, drew his hand out and stood against the wall.

Rollison put his gun away.

'Rollison,' the man said, 'there's just one way you can get out of this alive.'

He meant that.

His pale-grey eyes had a look that wasn't good. Here was a cold, calculating killer – and he must be desperate now.

'Do tell me,' said Rollison, 'I'm always interested in living.'

'Then you'd better listen carefully. I want—'

'By the way, where's Marion? Or do you always call her Lizzie?'

The man's teeth clamped together; the muscles of his cheeks worked.

'The girl stole some keys and an address – I want them,' the man said. 'She knows where they are. You can make her talk.'

'Won't she talk to you?'

'I'm in a hurry.'

'Well, well,' murmured Rollison, 'I thought you were friends with our Liz. I take it you killed Keller.'

'Never mind who killed Keller.'

'Oh, but I do,' said Rollison.

The man thrust his head forward, and his right hand dropped to his pocket. So did Rollison's. They stood watching each other, cat and mouse, and rage sparked from those cruel light-grey eyes.

'You don't get it, Rollison. If you make the girl talk, you've a chance. If you don't – I'll kill you myself, or send that witness to the police. Don't forget it. I want the keys and the address.'

'All right,' said Rollison lightly. 'Where is she?'

'In the next room.'

The man crossed the room and opened a door, put his hand inside and pulled down a switch. A dim light showed in the other room – either from a low-powered lamp or one with paper or cloth tied round it to lessen its brilliance. He stood on one side, and his right hand was still close to his pocket.

'Come here,' he said.

Rollison pushed his chair back, keeping his right hand near his gun. He moved, watching the man, whom he trusted as far as he would a rattlesnake. He reached the doorway of the next room, still watching; the other didn't move for his gun.

Rollison backed into the room. Pale eyes glittered at him. As he went farther, he saw that this was a bedroom. There was an oak wardrobe, pale carpet, a dressing-table against a heavily curtained window – then the foot panel of a single bed. He was by the side of the bed. He saw a girl's legs, bare, the feet lying limp. As he drew farther back, more of her legs came into sight; she wasn't fully dressed.

The legs were long, slender, shapely – as he'd seen before, when Marion-Liz had lazed on the Devon beach. They had the golden tan of the sun on them – but not at one spot, between the knee and thigh. There, the tan had been burned away; a small round burn showed, raw and ugly.

XIII

CRUSHED BEAUTY

ROLLISON couldn't look at both the girl and the man.

He backed farther away, taking swift glances at Marion-Liz. She wore a pair of green French knickers and a brassière; nothing else, except for a narrow leather belt round her waist. There were other burns on her body. Rollison felt rage blazing up inside him, a murderous fury, and his right arm flexed, he had to fight to keep his hand out of his pocket.

He had to choose between studying the girl and watching the man.

The man wanted the keys and that information desperately, here was living, livid proof. He thought Rollison could make the girl talk, and so wasn't likely to take drastic action – yet. He'd take that, once Rollison got what he wanted. So Rollison turned to look at Marion-Liz.

Her face wasn't touched.

There she lay in all her slender beauty, pale as a cream rose, limp, her spirit crushed – but her eyes wide open. Dread showed in them. The leather belt was tied by rope to the sides of the bed; the rope disappeared beneath the mattress. She could move a little but not get up. She didn't look as if she had the spirit to try to get up. Her hair had lost its glossy sheen, but was still attractive as it lay on the pillow, spread out like a dark halo. She closed her eyes when she recognized him, and shivered.

'Hallo, Liz,' said Rollison softly. 'I told you that you chose the wrong kind of friends.'

'Cut the talk,' the man said.

'Ah, yes,' said Rollison, and turned to face him. He closed his eyes, actually swayed on his feet. 'Not a pretty sight. If she won't talk after this, how do you expect me to make her?'

He looked at the man through his lashes; and he gulped, as if he felt sick.

'She said she wouldn't talk because you'd see her through, and now she knows you can't. What the hell's the matter with you? Can't you take it?'

'Never was good at this,' mumbled Rollison. 'I can take it when it comes quickly, but not like this.'

He actually staggered and put a hand on the bed, as if to steady himself, and the man took a step forward.

Rollison leapt at him, a darting fury. His fists worked liked pistons – smashing into the nose, the chin, the stomach. The man gasped and made strangled noises, tried to cover up, and hadn't a chance. Rollison smashed a swing to the side of his jaw and sent him reeling against the wall, followed it with a blow to the stomach that had every ounce of a hundred and seventy pounds behind it. The man with light-grey eyes gave a whining groan, doubled up, and lay in a heap.

Rollison drew back, but didn't speak.

He clenched his teeth as he bent down, took the gun away, ran through the other's pockets and found a second gun and a knife. He put them into his own pocket. He took keys and a wallet, too, and with these in his hands, backed away from his victim.

He was sweating.

He turned to Marion-Liz, and a smile broke through

the bleak mask of his face as he spread a sheet over her.

'All right, Liz, don't worry any more.'

The dread had gone; hope blazed.

'Just take it easy,' he said.

He used the man's knife to cut the ropes, had two long pieces, and went to his victim and pulled at him until he lay on his back, then tied his wrists and ankles. The man wasn't unconscious, but the power to resist had been hammered out of him. His lips were swollen, and there was a trickle of blood at one corner of his mouth. Rollison stood back, went to a hand-basin, ran cold water and rinsed his face and hands. He soaked a sponge, squeezed most of the water out, and went across to Liz. He bathed her eyes and face, then her hands; they were hot and clammy.

'Like to sit up?'

'I – can't.'

'Can't?'

'He did something to my back.'

Rollison didn't speak, but eased the girl up and turned the pillows over. He fetched water in a tooth-glass, raised her head and watched the eagerness with which she drank.

'Had anything to eat and drink?'

'No.'

'Just take it easy, Liz. Who is he?'

'His name is Woolf. He—' She broke off. 'I once worked with him.'

'All right,' said Rollison.

He went out of the room. He found other doors, and one led to a kitchen, but he didn't want to put on the light, that would probably be seen outside. He found the windows; a blind was drawn. He shone his torch,

and saw that the single lamp had been covered with a
piece of green cloth, there was no risk of the light
shining out. He opened the larder door and found an
open tin of unsweetened condensed milk, put on a
kettle, brewed strong tea, poured in plenty of the
milk and stirred in a lot of sugar. This took him five or
six minutes. He went back with a cup of tea, and the
man stared up at him, but didn't try to speak.

Rollison put an arm round the girl's neck, raised her
head, and held the cup for her. She sipped eagerly, but
before she had finished half the tea, she shook her head.
He put the cup on the bedside table, and then in-
spected the contents of the wallet. There were several
visiting-cards, reading:

Leo Woolf,
27 Mayrick Court,
Williton Street,
London, W.1.

He slipped these into his pocket and went through the
rest of the contents. A driving-licence, an identity card,
other oddments all bearing the same name and address,
he put back. There were six five-pound notes and
several one-pound notes. Stamps and two unused
railway tickets to Exeter made up the rest. He went
back to the man, felt in his pockets again, turned him
over so that he could get at his hip pockets. He found
nothing else of any use or value, nothing else with a
name on.

Marion-Liz muttered something, and Rollison didn't
catch the words. He went across to her; if he stood near
Woolf much longer, he wouldn't be able to keep his
hands off the man. He felt as if he were suspended in

mid-air, it was so utterly unlike what he had expected that he'd no plans to meet the situation – except the obvious. He could call the police in, show them the burns, let them force the truth out of Leo Woolf. But would that work?

'What is it, Liz?' He was very gentle.

'Be – careful,' she said. The fear was back in her eyes, the hope was fading. 'He'll have a man who'll – swear – you and I killed Keller.'

'A liar's no witness.'

'He will be. Can you – get us away?' Liz asked hoarsely.

There was something the matter with her back, which meant she couldn't walk. Woolf certainly wouldn't walk where he was told to go. The only way out of here was through the flat upstairs and the skylight.

Woolf sneered, 'Why don't you go and call the police in, Rollison? They're your friends, aren't they? Try it – and see what happens.'

Rollison sat on the side of the bed.

'You'll get seven years at least for this. Looking forward to it?'

'I shan't *hang*.'

He was sure of himself, and probably had cause to be.

'Listen, Rollison, I left word about what was to be done if the police caught up with me. Maybe I'll take a rap for what I've done to her, but she killed Keller, and you stood by and watched. Don't make any mistake about it, you're tight in that vise. Keller's throat was cut, first, with a knife. *Your* knife. I've got it in a safe place, with Keller's blood and your dabs on the handle.'

It was like hearing the sentence of death.

'Maybe *I'll* go to the police,' Woolf sneered. 'It would be worth seven years to know you went for the long drop.'

Rollison took out cigarettes, lit two, put one to the girl's lips, drew on the other and stood up – and startled them both, for he was smiling as if amiably.

'So that's where my knife went. You've chosen the wrong man for the drop, Leo, I've booked that for you. What's all this about?'

'As if you didn't know.'

'Just tell me.'

Woolf said, 'She knows where the Riordon stuff is, half a million pounds' worth. She knows where the keys are, too. I worked with her father. He got the stuff away – but she double-crossed me.'

Rollison didn't look round.

'True, Liz?'

She didn't answer.

'Is it true, Liz?'

She drew a deep breath.

'Not – not the way he puts it. He was blackmailing my father, made him get the Riordon jewels. I discovered it at the last minute. I'd learned that he was going to betray father to the police. I don't know where the stuff's hidden or where the keys are. I'm looking for the keys. I want to get everything and have the money waiting when my father comes out. That's – the truth.'

'Half a million pounds' worth,' mused Rollison. 'And one of your big mistakes, Liz, the law is hard to cheat. Forget the Riordon stuff. I think the simple thing is to have the police in, and force a showdown.'

'No!' cried Liz.

Woolf sneered, but wasn't happy.

'Try it,' he said. 'Just see what happens. Can't you understand plain English, Rollison? If the police get me, a witness will volunteer a statement about Keller. A friend of Keller's who was at the village by appointment. Don't make any mistake about it – his evidence will stand. He'll have good reasons for not coming forward before. I didn't take any chances when I was dealing with you, I knew this frame-up couldn't fail. And it won't. Do it the easy way. Make her tell you where the Riordon stuff is, and where the keys are. Then the witness won't show up.'

'And what about the other evidence you planted? Where's the girl who passed for Liz? How did you get the finger-prints on the spanner?'

Woolf chuckled, throatily, but more at ease – as if he sensed that Rollison was beginning to wilt.

'She handled it, before we used it. Never mind who the girl was. She wore Liz's shoes and Liz's dress, and she answered to the same description. You could tell them apart all right, but that doesn't matter. Forget her. There's one way out for you, and I've told you all about it. Cut these ropes off me, and get busy.'

Rollison didn't speak.

Liz said, 'Rolly.' The word sounded like a sigh, and her eyes were closed. 'He's too much for us, he's too thorough.'

'She's dead right,' sneered Woolf.

When he stopped, there was silence – and into the silence there came sounds, a long way off, but from inside the house. A man was hurrying up the stairs, and reached the landing outside. All three stared towards the door, and the girl was holding her breath. Woolf's eyes reflected fear again, and his teeth were bared.

A bell rang shrilly, and a man whispered at the front door – words which weren't distinguishable in here.

Rollison moved swiftly, into the dining-room and then into the tiny hall. The bell rang again. The police had seen whoever had come, might use this as a signal to close in.

The man whispered urgently, 'Elizabeth, open the door, let me in. I must see you – let me in.'

It was Reginald Rowse.

XIV

SUDDEN DEATH

Rowse paused for a moment, then whispered again, and kept his finger on the bell. The ringing sound from the kitchen seemed very loud.

Was he alone?

Was this a police trick?

Rollison couldn't see Rowse helping the police to catch Marion-Liz; couldn't see any reason why the police should send him. But he could understand them letting him come in; if he entered, they would follow and try to overhear whatever was said.

Well, they were the likely tactics.

'Liz! Let me in, it's urgent.'

Rollison didn't answer; there was no sound from the bedroom, only the ringing from the kitchen. Then that stopped. Rowse thudded on the door with his fist, making it shake.

If he came in, the police would soon be here.

If he left thinking the place was empty, they'd probably wait for other callers.

'Liz!' cried Rowse in a louder voice.

Anyone waiting downstairs would hear that.

Rollison opened the door abruptly, gripped Rowse's left wrist and drew him inside. Rowse gasped and staggered. Rollison closed the door, slipped the catch home again, said, 'Wait!' and hurried into the bedroom, grabbing a chair. He pushed this beneath the handle of the front door; it would take some time to break the door open.

Rowse straightened up, and spoke hoarsely. Dim light from the room beyond showed him vaguely.

'R-Rollison!'

Rollison gripped his arms and led him into the bedroom.

Rowse caught sight of Marion-Liz, and his muscles went rigid. The sheet hid her body and the scars, but couldn't hide her fear or pallor. Then he saw Woolf, and backed, hitting against Rollison.

'What *is* all this?'

'Listen to me, and don't lose your head. I've a job to do without police help. Liz is hurt, and can't get away. Nor can our Mr. Woolf – know him?'

'I've done a little business with him. Not much.'

'You won't do any more. He's going to produce a witness to swear that Liz killed Keller.'

'Why, I—' Rowse went beetroot red, clenched his fist, and strode forward. Rollison grabbed his arm and pulled him back. 'Let me get at him!'

He tried to free himself.

'Not yet. I want him out of here.'

It wasn't possible to get him out; forget it. That was another way of saying, 'Forget that he has the knife with my finger-prints and Keller's blood on it.' His tone didn't change as he went on:

'Remember that Liz might be hanged if you do the wrong thing. The police will come after I've gone. If they don't, go and fetch them – they're watching. You came, found the door opened under pressure, they'll believe that when they look at the lock. You talked to Liz, realized that as she can't move freely, the only thing was to give her up.'

Rowse's face was still a flaming red.

'Be damned to you! I can't do it, I won't do it!'

'All right. Let her hang.'

Woolf's light-grey eyes held desperation and un-certainty, Liz stared tensely at Rollison, Rowse raised his hands, as if to say that he didn't know what to make of it.

'How – how will it help?'

'When I've got Woolf away, I can get at the truth. Don't worry about how, I'll—'

He stopped.

He heard a movement at the door of the bedroom, and swung round, his hand at his pocket. He couldn't believe that the police had forced their way in silently. His heart raced – and then he saw a small man, hand-kerchief drawn up over his face and nose, gun in his right hand wrapped in another handkerchief.

The man fired – *at Woolf.*

The gun made a soft sneeze of sound. A small hole appeared on Woolf's forehead, Woolf made a coughing noise; then a rattle sounded in his throat. The little man swung round, slammed the door – and turned the key in the lock.

*　　*　　*

Rowse cried, 'You fool, you should have shot him!'

He rushed to the door.

Rollison said, 'Take it easy.'

He had to take it easy, and face new facts, which had come like a flash of lightning. New and damning facts – creating a new situation. Woolf wasn't the only one in this murderous game. The small man had come deliberately to kill him. The man had obviously been hiding in the flat; Rollison hadn't searched for anyone else – his one mistake, and a vital one.

The shot had made little noise; unless the police were on the landing, they probably hadn't heard it.

Rowse was quivering with rage, the girl staring in horror at the dead man.

Rollison went to the door, used a picklock and opened it cautiously. The door leading to the landing was open, the chair lay on its side. So the killer was prepared to run the gauntlet of the police. Then he heard a cry – another.

'*Hold him!*'

'*Careful!*'

Rowse grabbed Rollison's arm.

'You fool, they'll be here any minute, they – look!'

He pointed, and the light was good enough to show the air-pistol, lying on the red carpet of the dining-room. Footsteps thudded on the stairs.

Rollison closed and locked the hall door, put the chair into position again, then drew Rowse inside the dining-room and locked that door.

'Listen, Rowse, and don't make any mistakes. Tell them exactly what happened – exactly, understand?'

He heard a man shouting, 'He killed him, I saw him!'

He?

Was the little man saying Rollison had killed Woolf?

'I tell you it was Rollison!'

Liz cried in a moaning voice, 'What shall we do, what shall we do?'

'Just tell them the simple truth,' said Rollison. 'All that Woolf threatened, all he did – and what the little man did. But don't let them in yet.'

He picked up Woolf's wallet, with everything which gave the man's name, and turned to the window.

'Put out the light.'

Men were in the room next door, now, thudding on this door. A voice was raised, *'Open in the name of the law.'* It was absurd, and it was deadly. The certain thing was that if he were caught, he would be remanded in custody. There would be fending and proving – and there was a deadly witness against both him and Marion-Liz, a witness who might still speak.

'They'll be in the street,' Rowse gasped.

Men thudded against the outer door, and it creaked.

Rollison said again, 'Put out that light!'

Rowse obeyed, and Rollison pulled back the curtains, making little sound; that little was muffled by the noise at the door. It was a sash-cord window, and the room faced the street. He pushed the window up. The door creaked again, and Rowse trundled something heavy towards it. Rollison stood at the side of the window and looked out – and saw a uniformed constable on the pavement below. Light streamed out from a house opposite; Grice's men had been over there, had left their hiding-place.

The constable was staring at the front door.

Rollison climbed out of the window, groped with his feet and found a foot-hold on the ledge above the window below. He lowered himself gradually. A drain-pipe was close by, and he was able to get some support from it. There was a long drop, even from the top of this ground-floor window, and a pavement below; nothing to break a fall. He leaned sideways, putting most of his weight on the drain-pipe, and his hands came upon a union. That gave him a firm hold. He moved one leg, and put it on the union below, then took the chance and clung to the drain-pipe.

He couldn't see the constable now, and didn't hear a sound.

He slithered down. The Riley was waiting. Rollison let in the clutch and drove off, straight ahead, took the next right, then a left turn. He turned into a main road, feeling much cooler and calmer. The call wouldn't be out for a few minutes yet. The police would find the dead Woolf, and if they knew who he was, would soon be at 27 Mayrick Court.

How soon?

Mayrick Court was a block of modern flats, behind Park Lane.

Rollison stopped the car five minutes' walk from the flats, and hurried along the deserted streets. Only a few cars passed, and one or two taxis, with their lighted signs up.

A night porter was on duty, and the entrance to the flats was discreetly lighted. The hall was also dimly lit, with concealed wall lighting. The porter was sitting at a table, looking at some magazines. He got up quickly.

Rollison said, 'Good evening, I've an appointment with Mr. Woolf.'

'I *think* he's out, sir.'

'I'll go and see – someone will be in, I take it?'

'Oh, yes – Mrs. Woolf and the maid.'

'Thanks.'

'I'll take you up,' said the porter, and headed for the lift; the light in there would be bright, they would be at close quarters.

'I'll walk, thanks, it's only the first floor, isn't it?'

'Second floor, sir.'

'I'll still walk.'

Rollison nodded and went towards the stairs. He didn't glance round, but felt that the man was staring after him. With natural curiosity, or because he had recognized him? Rollison stopped just round the corner, and crept back.

The porter sat down at the table again.

Rollison hurried up the carpeted stairs. How long had he before the police arrived here? Ten minutes? More – or less. He'd taken everything by which Woolf would be easily recognized. Would Rowse and Marion-Liz have the nerve to stall? If they did, identification might take an hour or more, even longer.

He reached the second floor.

A wide passage stretched to the right and left, with carpeted floors, recesses, discreet wall lighting. The flats were luxurious, almost palatial. There were no directing notices. He turned right, passed Numbers 23 and 21, turned back and found Number 27 the second door on the left.

He stood outside, listening.

He heard no sound.

He took out Woolf's keys, selected one Yale and tried it; it didn't open the door. The second key did. Rollison pushed the door open gently, and stepped into darkness, relieved only by the light behind him.

He closed the door, making a slight sound, and stood listening again. Woolf's wife and maid should be here; but he saw no light under any of the doors. He switched on the hall light.

The hall was rectangular, spacious, with a few expensive water-colours on the walls. Several doors led off it, painted gold; five, in all. He went to the nearest, opened it, and saw a bedroom with a woman asleep on one of twin beds. She didn't stir. He took the key from the inside, closed and locked the door, and tried again.

He found himself in a book-lined room, a study or library.

He locked all the other doors so that he couldn't be taken by surprise from inside the flat now. He went back to the front door, and jammed a chair beneath the handle, then he turned towards the book-lined room. Woolf was most likely to keep records and papers in here.

He wanted to find the girl who had passed herself off as Marion-Liz. Once he could do that –

He went across to a large pedestal desk, a luxurious piece in walnut; everything here was walnut, and the walls were panelled. He switched on a desk-light, then sat at the desk and began to try the keys.

XV

POLICE PROGRESS

The telephone bell woke Grice, just after twelve-thirty.

He grunted and stretched out a hand, eyes heavy with sleep. He opened one, but there was no light.

'Grice speaking.'

'Middleton here, I'm at Hilton Street. Can you—'

'Have you got him?' Grice started up.

'Just missed him,' Middleton said, 'but we've got the girl. And another body.'

Grice didn't speak.

'Did you hear?' asked Middleton.

'Yes. Not the girl?'

'She's in a bad way, but alive. Rowse is here, too, getting hysterical. I'd like to have another go at him while he's like that. Will you come?'

'Yes.'

Grice put down the receiver and jumped out of bed, now wide awake. He flung on some clothes and left his bachelor flat ten minutes after he'd said 'yes'.

Several constables stood outside the house in Hilton Street, and made way for him to enter. A plain-clothes man was in the hall, and lights blazed from all the rooms. The downstairs neighbours were up, a man stood at the open door, questions in his eyes. Grice went straight up, and found Middleton in the little dining-room. A police-surgeon was here, Grice saw

him bending over a bed in the next room, but couldn't
see who was on it.

Rowse was sitting at the table, his hands clenched
and his lips compressed.

'Well?' asked Grice.

'He's being difficult,' Middleton said almost casually.

'Difficult!' cried Rowse. 'I've told you everything I
can. You damned police! All you do is make mistakes,
thundering big mistakes, and look what you've let them
do to Liz. Go and look!' he shouted, and his eyes were
bloodshot, his cheeks pale, a curiously milky colour.
'Go and see what the devil did to her while you were
waiting outside! Go on! See how proud you'll be!'

'What's this?' Grice asked.

Middleton said, 'It's true, I'm afraid. There was a
man with her. He'd burned her with cigarette-ends, to
try to make her talk. She's unconscious – nothing
phoney about it.'

'If you'd raided the flat earlier, it wouldn't have
happened,' sobbed Rowse.

Grice looked at him levelly.

'Supposing you get yourself in hand, then—'

'Don't you talk to me like that.' Rowse clenched his
fists, looked hysterical with rage. 'You remember you're
a public servant, I pay your wages. Pay you for letting
a devilish thing like this happen to a girl who—'

He choked, and tears sprang to his eyes.

'Wait downstairs for me, Mr. Rowse, will you?'

'I damned well won't! I want to know what you're
going to do with Miss Lane.'

Grice went to the door and called, 'Sergeant!'

A uniformed sergeant came hurrying.

'Take Mr. Rowse downstairs, have him wait for me,'

Grice said. 'Come along, Rowse, I've too much to do to listen to hysterical young men.'

He took Rowse's arm.

Rowse hit out and caught Grice a glancing blow, near enough the bruise on his chin to hurt.

Grice said, 'That'll do. Charge him with assault, Sergeant, and hold him at Cannon Row.'

'Why, you devil, you—'

'Come along, now.'

The sergeant was massive, and had a soothing voice and a powerful grip. Rowse started to struggle, but gave it up.

The police-surgeon, bald as a billiard ball, with pink and shiny face, came in from the bedroom.

'About time someone took that young man in hand,' he said.

'Thanks. What's doing?'

'The corpse is very much a corpse. Air-pistol slug fired at fairly close quarters, and death was instantaneous. The girl—' He shrugged. 'She isn't badly hurt, unless the trouble in her back is serious. It's badly bruised, looks as if she had a kick. She's unconscious. I've sent for an ambulance, and we'll get her straight to hospital.'

'When can she talk?'

The police-surgeon shrugged.

'Maybe tomorrow, maybe she'll be semi-conscious for days.'

Men were coming up the stairs, and the door was opened by a man in a long white coat, one of two ambulance men who came in briskly. The police-surgeon led them into the bedroom. He pulled back the sheet, to show Grice some of the scars.

Photographers and finger-print men were busy; they'd finished with the girl, were now starting the routine on the man's body. Middleton joined Grice.

'Let me have it all,' Grice said. 'Identified the man?'

'No, and there's nothing in his pockets,' said Middleton. 'I can give you everything I know, sir. Rowse came here, about an hour ago. One of our men followed him to the foot of the stairs. He kept whispering for the girl, then disappeared. Our man stayed where he was – on instructions. Rowse would have been picked up as he left. But there was trouble we didn't expect. Apparently two men were in the flat, as well as the Lane girl. This chap and a smaller man, who's at the station. The smaller man, Nevett, says that Rollison was here, and did the shooting.'

Grice's eyebrows went up.

'Using an air pistol?'

'I'm telling you what Nevett said. As a story, it could stand up. He and this chap have been here all the time, they came on the night Keller was killed. He won't give the dead man's name. Rollison arrived—'

'How?'

'Front door of the flat.'

Grice said thinly, 'Rowse has got something. What do we get paid for?'

The sharp edge of anger was in his voice.

'No one came in at the back or the front,' Middleton said, 'and that left the roof. I've had a man up there. No doubt Rollison came in through the skylight, it's been forced open. The people in the top flat aren't home yet, they went out early in the evening. Rollison came through there and down the stairs and forced the lock. The usual mica job, he can do that standing on his head.'

'I know Rollison's capability. Go on.'

Grice's voice was like a whip, and Middleton's face completely blank. The photographer finished and packed up his camera and tripod; two other men were taking measurements between the walls and the body on the floor.

'Nevett said Rollison was after him, and he ran. He couldn't get out by the street and ran upstairs, but we'd put a man up there by then.'

'Well, well,' said Grice. 'Someone must be brilliant.'

The sarcasm was searing.

Middleton didn't defend himself or the others.

'So we caught him, and he yelled about Rollison and a gun. The inside doors were locked, and one was barricaded. By the time we had it down, Rollison had gone through the window, avoided the man on duty in the street, and got off. He had a car waiting – a fairly new Riley. I've put a call out.'

'And when you've found it, how far away do you think Rollison will be?' Grice walked across to the dead man. 'Have you told them to get his picture round pretty quickly?'

'Yes – copies to the Press, first. I've a feeling I've seen him about somewhere,' Middleton went on. 'The Street might know him – and Records *might*.' He was obviously doubtful. 'That's most of it. Rowse said this was one address where he thought the girl might be and he'd called everywhere else, so tried this. Says he wasn't sure she was here. He also says that it wasn't Rollison but Nevett who shot this chap. The girl corroborated. They say they don't know the dead man.'

'What next?'

'That's about all,' said Middleton. 'We should have been prepared for Rollison to use the roof. And we should—'

'Have had that top flat watched all the time. Nevett went upstairs, you say?'

'Yes.'

'He might have been going to hide up there, the top flat could be rented by the same mob. We'll break in—'

'We've been in.'

'All right, we'll search thoroughly, and I'll get the warrant,' said Grice. 'Check the tenants as soon as you can. And get this man identified.' He stood looking down at Woolf, whose features were slack, in death, and whose eyes were only partly closed. 'Yes, I've seen him about.' He snapped his fingers impatiently. 'It's beginning to look as if we were right one way, anyhow – the girl knows where the Riordon stuff is. Have you questioned her about that yet?'

'Haven't had a chance.'

Grice shrugged.

He checked over everything that had been done, left Middleton in charge, and went to the Yard. It was nearly half past two, and he wouldn't get home again that night. Prints of the photograph of the dead man were already on his desk, damp but usable. Copies were on the way to newspapers, and Records were being searched for a photograph and for finger-prints to correspond with those which had been taken from the dead man. He telephoned to the Back Room Inspector and released the story of the girl's arrest.

Middleton came in, poker-faced, eyes heavy and tired, but his movements and voice were brisk enough.

'Sit down,' Grice said.

'Thanks. I'm damned sorry about this.'

'Can't be helped. You're not the only one Rollison's shown a clean pair of heels. I wish I knew what the devil he's up to. Let's go over this again. He was there talking to the girl, let Rowse in, and before there could be any more discussion, the little man arrived. Had he been hiding in the flat?'

'Yes. In a corner cupboard in the dining-room.'

'If Rowse is right, he came out and shot the unknown, with two witnesses,' Grice said. 'Then he blames Rollison.'

Middleton said heavily, 'Listen, Chief. We know that girl killed Keller. Rollison's trying to cover her. Rowse is crazy about her, so they'd all lie like troopers. We can take Nevett's word as safely as theirs. There are no prints on the air-pistol, so that doesn't mean anything. There's nothing to help us.'

Grice shrugged.

'Which means we should have to believe that Rollison shot the unknown in cold blood.' Middleton shook his head slowly. 'I can't see it happening. Can you?'

'Not the Rollison I know,' Grice said.

The telephone bell rang. He lifted the receiver quickly, and snapped his name.

He listened. His eyes glistened, and his hand tightened on the receiver.

He barked, 'You sure?' He paused, listening again, then said, 'Yes, send a call out, all patrol cars in the vicinity to go there.' He banged the receiver down and jumped up. Middleton was already on his feet, something of the tiredness fading from his eyes.

'We've identified the dead man – a Leo Woolf, of 27 Mayrick Court, Mayfair,' Grice said. 'Let's get over there. Remember where we've seen that man before?'

'No, I—'

'Witness during the girl's father's trial. Not a case we worked on, but I once saw him in court. Reputedly wealthy, married a chorus girl a few years ago. Come on.'

XVI

WOOLF'S STUDY

THE third key Rollison tried opened the middle drawer in Woolf's desk. Two of the side drawers remained locked. He found the keys for them, pulled each drawer open, and glanced inside. The middle drawer held a blotting-pad, pens and pencils, oddments. Another contained notepaper and envelopes; everything was very tidy.

In the first of the smaller locked drawers were an address-book, several account-books, confidential papers. He put these on one side, and tried the other. In it were several manilla folders; in one of these were photographs of several people, including Marion-Liz and Harry Keller. Rollison glanced at the murdered man's round pudge of a face, put the photograph aside and studied the others. He knew several of them. Names were written in pencil on the back – and the first name to ring a bell was Nathaniel Lane – Solicitor.

Marion-Liz's father looked elderly, amiable, and benevolent, a grey-haired, full-faced man with tufts of hair at his temples and bushy eyebrows.

Then Reginald Rowse grinned up at him, looking more Irish in the photograph than he did in real life.

The police could draw their own conclusions from this. Rollison wanted only that knife.

He opened the last drawer. Inside were two automatics and some spare clips of ammunition, and a much smaller gun. This could be held in the palm of the hand and remain unnoticed, but could be lethal.

He stood up and looked round the room, for the safe.

One long wall, opposite the heavily curtained windows, was filled with books. The glazed shelves were built to the height of the picture-rail at either end, but went only half-way up the wall between these ends. On the top shelf of the lower section were several ornaments. The room was furnished tastefully, obviously belonging to a man who could put his hands on plenty of money.

At one end was a fireplace, easy-chairs, low tables; nothing there concealed a safe, unless it was behind a picture. That would mean a wall combination safe.

He went across to the window and pulled a curtain aside cautiously, opened a window wide, and then put the curtain back, so that only a sliver of light showed outside. He turned to the end of the room which he hadn't examined closely. The door through which he had entered was here, and against the wall behind it, a large cabinet. Cocktails? He went across and opened the top part; yes, bottles and glasses were fitted into little partitions, a neat and attractive array, but they didn't take up the whole of the cabinet. He tried to open the door in the bottom part; it was locked.

He used a small key from Woolf's bunch, and the door sagged open. The safe lay behind it. The knife, too?

There were two keyholes, one very small; and there was a long, thin key which fitted it. The safe was unfamiliar; in some makes it was necessary to use the correct key first, if the wrong one were turned it jammed the second lock. He examined the long key carefully, but there was no marking on it. He tried

those keys he hadn't yet used, until he found one that
appeared to fit the second lock – the only one, and
therefore almost certainly the correct one. He drew it
out without turning it and examined it closely, but
found no markings. Woolf would know which one to
use first, there was no reason why there should be any
indication. He went closer to the safe door itself and
peered at the dull-finished steel, sometimes the locks
themselves were marked.

These weren't.

'Can I help you?' asked a woman.

*   *   *

Rollison straightened up slowly, and didn't look
round. The 'can I help you' seemed to ring in his ears
louder than an alarm bell, but he checked the rise of
panic and the temptation to feel for his gun. He saw a
reflection in a picture on the wall above the cabinet,
but could only see the vague outline of a woman's
head and shoulders.

'Don't be shy,' she said.

She had a pleasant voice, deep, slightly husky. He
expected to see beauty. He turned, slowly, and his lips
curved in a smile, showing nothing of his thumping
heart.

She stood quite still, dressed in a royal blue dressing-
gown which was waisted and very square on the
shoulders, and showed only a shallow 'V' at the neck.
It touched the floor; the toes of red slippers poked
beneath it. The skirt was full and fell in heavy folds
about her.

She wasn't young; not really young; but she was
superb to look at.

Behind her, one of the tall sections of the bookshelves was open a few inches; the shelves concealed a door.

She had dark hair, with a streak of grey which started at the forehead and was swept back. Her hair fell to her shoulders in waves; not natural, but did that matter? Her complexion was lovely; she had on a little make-up.

'Mr. Rollison, I presume,' she said. 'Will you have a drink?'

'No, thanks.'

'Then have a cigarette.'

She backed to a table, and with her left hand, groped for a cigarette from a box. She held an automatic pistol in her right hand. She took the cigarette and then a lighter from the table, flicked it into flame, and drew on the tobacco. Then she backed a little farther away and motioned him to the box. He moved across and lit a cigarette, the keys jangling in his hand.

'Where did you get those keys?'

'Just my luck,' murmured Rollison. 'Didn't anyone tell you that I was born under a lucky star?'

'I've never had much time for astrology, and you shouldn't have, now. Supposing I were to telephone for the police – they'd be delighted.'

'And you would have done your civic duty.'

'That's right. Have you any objection?'

Rollison laughed and waved his right hand.

'None at all, carry on.'

She didn't move towards the telephone, which was behind her.

'Perhaps it wouldn't be to our mutual advantage,' said Rollison earnestly. 'Possibly you've a black past, too. You wouldn't be Mrs. Woolf, would you?'

She smiled at that, as if she really thought it funny – an unexpected reaction from a wife hearing a slur on her husband, unless she sailed through life ready and eager to be amused at anything. The glint in her eyes wasn't just of amusement; there was malice in it.

'I am Mrs. Woolf,' she said.

'Now we know each other, what could be cosier?'

'What do you want?'

'Oh, just an odd thing or two – proof that Leo has been murdering people, and all that kind of thing.'

'And you think he would keep it in his safe?'

She made no denial, but the laughter in her eyes was touched with venom. Towards whom? She was superbly confident, and that was partly her nature, not all due to the gun in her hand. She went to a chair and sat down, but all the time the gun covered him. He believed that she would shoot as readily as Woolf had done; and probably to kill.

'Useful things, safes,' said Rollison. 'The odd thing is that so many people think they are. Safe, I mean. Men have a pathetic faith in them – even clever crooks. They seem to have the notion that only their own safes are safe from burglars.'

'Perhaps they do. What exactly do you want?'

'The name of the girl friend who was at Hexley on Wednesday night. Was Leo out of town?'

She didn't answer.

'You wouldn't know where he is now, would you?' asked Rollison.

He tapped the ash off his cigarette, and rested his right hand at his waist; he had only to slide his hand into his pocket to get at his gun.

'Don't you know?' she asked.

He smiled, and didn't answer.

'Where is Leo?' She was obviously striving to keep back anger, the smile was as much pose as anything else. 'You must have seen him, to get his keys.'

What would she say, if she knew that he was dead?

'Oh, I saw him,' he said. 'We had an interesting chat. It was a pity the girl was with us, I think he would have been more frank if he'd been alone, but—'

She spat, 'What girl?'

'I wouldn't know her name. A very nice young lady, I should say, and—'

The woman's eyes blazed with anger. She was aware of Wolf's *affaires*, was fiercely jealous. Could that be the explanation of the strange light in her eyes?

'Where is he?'

'Oh, still around, I expect.'

'How did you get the keys?'

Rollison rubbed his chin and said apologetically, 'I'm afraid I was unkind. He annoyed me, and I hit him. Look.' He held out his left hand; the knuckles were slightly grazed, there was a smear of blood on two of them. 'He was so surprised that he didn't hit back, and I had no trouble taking the keys away. I left him dismayed, but not very active. True, I don't think he'll have much regard for me in future, I'm always making bad friends. Men especially are allergic to me.'

'I can believe that,' she said. 'I can't believe that you did all that to Leo.'

'Oh, he's nothing like so good as he thinks he is.'

Rollison moved forward, casually.

'Don't come too close,' she warned.

For all he knew, the police had identified Woolf. The

sound of police cars might come through the open window at any moment. He had only limited time; and the safe might yield exactly what he wanted. But the woman was more dangerous than the man had been.

She wasn't in a hurry; she was likely to enjoy a cat-and-mouse game. She didn't know that Woolf was dead and that the police might arrive at any moment. But if he were too anxious, she would guess he was on edge.

'Oh, come,' he protested mildly, 'must we have guns, between friends? You offered to help – which key should be used first?'

'I don't know,' she said. 'I wish I did.'

'You know,' murmured Rollison, 'there are moments when I doubt if you're as closely attached to Leo as he would like to think. Why do you wish you did?'

'There is plenty I'd like to find in his safe.'

'Couldn't we strike a bargain?'

She didn't answer.

'After all, I could try,' said Rollison. 'I might choose the wrong one, and we'd be no farther on, but if I chose the right one, we could take what we want. Full satisfaction all round, I can't imagine we want exactly the same thing.' He lifted the long, thin key. 'Shall I try?'

'Yes,' she said.

XVII

THE SAFE

ROLLISON couldn't shut the glimpse of the woman's naked hatred out of his mind. He couldn't understand why she should say 'yes'. He didn't like turning with his back to her, for she might shoot.

He smiled, as if at a life-long friend.

'Or would you like to try? After all, it's more your safe than mine.'

'Open it,' she said harshly.

She didn't move from the arm of the chair. She was ten feet away from him, too far for him to hope to disarm her, unpleasantly close for accurate marksmanship; if she shot to kill, she could hardly miss.

He shrugged.

'Don't you want to come and see how it's done?'

'I want to see if you can do it.'

He turned slowly. He had a glimpse of her, steady and calm, gun-hand raised, the automatic now trained on his side.

He turned his back on her; and could hardly breathe.

There was no other sound.

He took three steps towards the safe, and felt as if his hair were standing on end. He was cold at the forehead and the nape of the neck, and his hands were clammy. He knelt down, slowly; it was like kneeling before the executioner's block.

She didn't move, and she didn't shoot.

He used the small key, first – then glanced round. She was leaning forward, so that she could see better, but the gun remained steady. At least, she really wanted him to open the safe. But what would happen when it was open? He could see the dark pit of death yawning in front of him. If he unlocked the safe, she could take out whatever she wanted – and if she shot him, she would have every reason. It was a legal act to shoot a man who had forced a way in and was opening one's safe.

He turned the key; there was a faint click, nothing to suggest that the lock hadn't turned. He slid the second in, and hesitated – and then turned with a quick twist of the fingers and coughed at the same time, to cover any sound. The key turned easily. All he had to do now was to pull at the handle of the safe, and it would open.

'What's the matter?' she asked abruptly.

'Open it – it's all yours.'

'Is it unlocked?'

'It is, if those keys will unlock it.'

'Open the door,' she ordered.

She was looking intently at him, and the smile had gone from her eyes, their expression was one of unholy expectation; she came forward a step.

He felt quite sure that once she knew that the door was open, she would shoot him. He felt like a sitting bird. He coughed again, overdoing it and going red in the face. He snatched at his pocket, as if for a handkerchief, bending down at the same time. He pulled out his gun and plunged forward.

She fired.

Her face was a twisted mask, and hatred glittered in her eyes. The bullet plucked at the carpet – and his leg.

He fired at her gun, and the whole of the future seemed to hang on that shot. It roared, flame flashed – and she cried out and flung her hand up. Her gun curved an arc, and hit the wall and dropped heavily to the floor. She clapped one hand about her wrist.

The echoes of the shots faded.

Rollison stood up and walked towards her gun, making no sound.

The window was open; and the maid was in the flat. The shots must have been heard. Yet the silence remained, tense as the moment before the crack of thunder. He picked her gun up and slipped it into his pocket, and she stood watching him, lips beginning to twitch. Otherwise, she didn't move. There was no blood; he'd hit the gun.

A voice sounded, 'Madame – madame, wake – *oh*!'

That was a scream, cut short; the maid was in the next room.

Rollison whispered, 'Talk to her.'

The maid had seen the empty bed, and the bookcase door was open an inch; that was why they could hear her. How had she got in? Rollison stepped close to the wall, covering the woman with his gun. She approached the bookcase door.

The maid began to gasp.

The woman said, 'Elsa, it's all right – I thought someone was in here, but I was wrong. Go back to bed.'

'Oh, madame!' The girl sobbed.

Mrs. Woolf went to the bookcase door, opened it wider, and spoke soothingly; she had complete control of herself again. She let her wrenched wrist fall to her side.

'It's all right, Elsa, go back to your room.'

Rollison saw a door in the next room – a communicating door from the woman's room to her maid's.

'Oh, madame, I *was* frightened!'

'Yes, I know, but there's no need to be.'

Rollison heard the maid's dragging footsteps; and then a door closed.

The woman shut the bookcase door.

She turned to face Rollison – and looked as she had done when he had first seen her. Superbly beautiful and smiling, as if that venomous rage had never existed. He began to wonder if she were sane; but would an insane person have been able to treat the maid like that?

There was no sound from the street; no police.

She said quietly, 'I think I'm beginning to believe in lucky stars, no one else seems to have heard that.'

'Next door—' Rollison began.

'They are away, for the summer, the flat is empty.'

'Upstairs?'

'We've heard nothing, and we could hear if anyone were moving about.' She glanced at the ceiling, then approached him, relaxed and smiling. 'You're better than I thought in some ways, but not so good in others, Toff. You're nervous.'

'That's right,' said Rollison. 'I don't like beautiful women who go about using guns – it kills my faith in human nature.'

'I should hate to do that. Aren't you going to look in the safe, now you've opened it?'

'No. You are.'

She shrugged, and went towards the safe, and he covered her. She had no gun, but he didn't trust her. There might be another gun in the safe. He moved so that he could see over her shoulder when she was kneeling down – and she had to kneel on one knee in order to pull at the handle.

He said, 'Wait a minute.'

She paused.

'If you and your husband have anything in common, it's devilishness,' he said. 'Keep to one side when you pull the door open.'

She looked round – and she seemed to be younger, almost a girl; her eyes were dancing with real amusement.

'Why? Are you still nervous?'

'I just don't trust Woolfs. Keep to one side, and pull the door slowly.'

She obeyed, so that she was facing him. In spite of her words, she was as nervous as he, seemed to have difficulty in plucking up her courage to pull the door open. She tugged; it was heavy, placed like that she couldn't get much force behind her arm. When it opened, it would swing towards her.

She pulled again.

The door opened – and a stab of flame hissed out, there was a coughing sound, followed by a dull thud at the other end of the room. A bullet buried itself in the panelling.

The woman knelt there, as if transfixed, staring at the door.

Rollison said softly, 'The old trick, trust Leo to think of it.'

He went across and stood by her side, convinced that for once she was completely dumbfounded, had been shocked to numbness. He was careful as he pulled the door wider open. Inside, at the top, the pistol had been rigged so that a shot was fired whenever the door was opened; he could see the little wire which ought to have been pushed to one side for the door to be opened without the shot being fired.

The safe stood wide open, at last.

The woman said, 'The – *devil*!'

She was shivering, and her voice quivered. She got up slowly, and leaned against Rollison. He kept his gun-hand free, but he didn't think there was any danger from her for a moment.

She drew her head back.

There was no sound outside, the shots hadn't been heard – but at any moment a car might turn the corner and pull up.

She said chokingly, 'I'll kill him. I'll kill him.'

'No love for Leo?'

'Love? I've hated him for years. He's fooled, tricked, and cheated me. He's humiliated me before my friends. He laughs and sneers and reviles me, and thinks I'll always come to heel. Well, he's wrong. He's been wrong for a long time, but he didn't know it. I'll break him – I'll kill him!'

What would she say if she knew that Woolf was dead?

'Why not humiliate him? Break him that way?' He smiled into her eyes. 'It would be easy, wouldn't it?'

She didn't answer.

'He's framed a girl for Keller's murder. Why not help to prove that he was behind it?'

The words came casually, he turned away.

'Save *her*? Not in a thousand years!'

He didn't speak.

'You fool, Rollison, you don't know him. He gets what he wants from every woman he likes, and then gets rid of them. Somehow – anyhow. That's what he thinks he's done with me. I'm just a cover for him, a cover of respectability, the good wife in the background. I'm too old for my fine Leo – much too old. He likes them young. This Lane girl – they had a wonderful time for a few weeks, she thought he was in love with her. She was one of those who helped to take him away. Help *her*? I'd gladly watch her hang.'

She stopped.

As he watched her, he heard a car approaching, some way off. It was the first sound he had heard from outside since he had come here. The noise set his nerves jangling, playing on them as if they were raw. He stared at the woman, and hoped that she would not notice the tension in him. The car slowed down and turned a corner – and came this way. He moved because the stillness was unbearable. It was almost outside, now.

It passed.

He took a whisky bottle from the cabinet.

'Have a drink,' he said. He ran his hand over his forehead, and it came away damp. 'Whisky – or brandy?'

He poured her a whisky, added a splash of soda, and handed it to her. She drank it almost without realizing what she was doing. He helped himself.

He lit cigarettes for them both.

'All right,' he said. 'Let the Lane girl hang. Leo will get away with that, as he's got away with everything else. And you'll have missed a chance to see him in the dock, to hear the judge pass sentence.'

She looked at him from smouldering eyes, but the red-hot flame of hatred had slackened a little. She forced a laugh, and moved away from him.

138

'What's the Lane girl mean to you?'

'Just a girl who's had a raw deal.'

'She couldn't have one raw enough. You don't know her. She's as hard as they're made. Bad, do you understand, bad right through. I know Elizabeth Lane.' She drew at her cigarette, and her recovery was almost complete, there was mockery in her eyes – and that unnatural glint. 'You've fallen for her, haven't you? You've risked your own neck to save hers. I wouldn't lift a finger to do that, but I *might* help you.'

He didn't speak.

'So you know Leo framed her. I wonder how well you know Leo. I wonder how you discovered that he was behind it. Oh, forget it, I don't care.' She went across to a chair, watching him. 'Why, you're handsome,' she said, as if surprised. 'Your photographs don't do you justice, they make you look too old.'

She was talking about photographs. The open safe was near him, and he was listening to her while he could be going through its contents. But he knew that she could tell him what he most wanted to know, she could prove that Woolf had framed Marion-Liz.

'You're not exactly an old hag yourself,' he said.

She laughed softly.

'But you prefer them young, like the Lane girl. Oh, don't lie, it's not worth lying. If he were gone, perhaps I could start to live again, but—'

She broke off.

Rollison said, 'Supposing we find out what's in the safe. What do you want from it?'

'Anything I can find about him,' she said, but the passion wasn't in her voice, she could switch that on and off; had it been acting all the time? Surely that wasn't possible. 'He's as corrupt as the Devil himself, and the secrets of that safe could damn him. If I can get them, I'll send him to hell. I'll make him writhe and squirm, I'll make him do what I want, I'll let him know what it's like to live the way I've lived. Open it. Take everything out.'

He turned, and bent down.

He didn't know what warned him, but glanced round at her – as a knife swept towards his back.

XVIII

THE MESSAGE

HE plunged forward. The knife, aimed at his ribs, slid softly into the flesh at his waist. He fell at full length, twisting round as he did so. She was off her balance, because of the plunging stab. He clutched her ankle and pulled, and she fell heavily on top of him. He heaved her off. She rolled on to the floor, without any attempt to struggle.

He stood up, and trod on the knife; the blade snapped.

'I don't think I like you, Mrs. Woolf,' he said softly. 'I don't think we'll get on at all well together.' He lifted her; she was heavy, but in this mood he could have thrown her bodily at the wall. He dropped her into an easy-chair, and pulled the sash from her waist. It was sewn on at one side, and he tore at it; the stitches broke. He gripped her hands and bound them together.

She sat glaring.

He went to the safe and knelt down. There were jewel-cases and legal documents in thick envelopes; deeds of property, most of them; bundles of share certificates, all the normal things. He put them aside. He took out two thin bundles of one-pound notes, tossed them away, and glanced into the now nearly empty safe.

There was one sealed envelope; and a small black book. No weapon, no knife.

He took out the book.

In it was a list of names and addresses; hundreds of names and addresses. Under each letter of the alphabet there were two sets of entries – men on one side, women on the other. There was no time to go through this. There were no notes against any of the entries, little that might give him a clue to anything he wanted.

He slipped the book into his pocket, and picked up the envelope. He felt it, but there were only papers inside.

A car drew near again.

He stood up, slowly, and strolled to the window, as if he weren't affected by it; but his heart started to thump again. He pulled the curtain aside an inch. The headlights of a car swept into the street.

It was nearly two o'clock.

He turned back, glanced at the woman, whose position hadn't changed, but whose face was blank and almost sullen. He started to tear open the envelope.

The telephone bell rang, breaking the silence.

It made them both start.

The bell kept on ringing with the steady regular ring of a local call. The telephone itself was on the desk. He approached it, stopping and pulling the woman up as he passed; she let herself be drawn up, and he spoke quietly.

'Is there an extension?'

'In the hall.'

He went across and opened the door; a telephone stood on a small table just outside. He went back, while the telephone bell kept ringing.

The police?

They would come straight here, this wasn't likely to be a police call.

He undid the sash at her wrists.

'Answer it, and be natural – I'm covering you.'

She might doubt whether he would shoot, might defy him. He backed away, keeping her covered, and she didn't even turn to look at him. She touched the telephone. He backed into the hall and lifted the receiver, and as he put it to his ear, the woman said:

'Hallo.'

A man answered; so she hadn't lied about the extension.

'Leah, listen to me,' the man said, in a breathless voice. 'He's dead.'

Rollison saw the woman's shoulders move, then she glanced round at him, her eyes blazing with an unholy light.

The man spoke urgently, 'Leah, did you hear me? He's dead. *Leo's* dead.'

She said in a strange, unnatural voice, 'Yes, I heard you. I don't believe it.'

'It's true. He was at Liz Lane's flat – he's been there all the time. Nevett was there, too. I traced Nevett tonight. He's under arrest.'

Rollison heard the sharp intake of Leah Woolf's breath.

'*Nevett* is? Did he—'

'I don't know. He says Rollison did the job. You know, Rollison – the Toff.'

She didn't glance over her shoulder, just said, 'Yes.'

Rollison took an envelope from his pocket and printed on it, in pencil, 'Ask if they've identified your husband.' It was awkward, trying to hold the paper steady with his elbow as he listened.

'I haven't been able to find out much,' the man said.

'The tenants in the flat above were in Leo's pay, he could go up and down as he pleased, as the police weren't inside the house. He sent the tenants out to-night, he wanted to work on the girl, and she might have been noisy. Nevett told me that, on the telephone. Can you hear me?'

'Yes.' Her voice was still tensely calm. 'Go on.'

'Rollison got in, somehow. There was trouble, and then Nevett blew up, I don't know exactly what happened. The police caught him. I've just been talking to a friend in Fleet Street. Nevett's on a charge, the police have got the girl and her boy friend. Rollison got away. He may visit you, be careful.'

She gave voice to a shocking sound that might have been a laugh.

'Leah, what's the matter?'

'I still don't believe you.'

'Listen, this is sober truth. Leo's dead – shot through the head. It's official, the police have released a story.'

Rollison put his instrument down softly, and strode across to the woman, thrust the envelope in front of her nose. She took it, and read. The man was still talking. Rollison went back and picked up his receiver.

'You'll be all right if you keep your head,' the man was saying, 'but we've got to get that safe open. We've got to save the records.'

She said, 'That won't be so easy. Jim, do the police know who he is?'

'Not yet. That gives us time. Listen, I've fixed up with a man to come over – Sammy Gilbert. He's reliable, and he can open any safe. Let him in, get him to open it, take out the papers we want. He'll be there soon, and knows what to do.'

'Why don't you come yourself, Jim?'

The man didn't answer.

Rollison felt tension easing its way out of him, like pain fading away. It was a quarter past two, and the police still didn't know who Woolf was; so they might not know until the morning, and probably wouldn't.

'Well, why don't you?' Leah Woolf asked the man on the telephone.

'There's no sense in taking risks. Let Sammy get the door open, give him the dope, and then it'll be fine. When the police come, you don't know anything about it. It won't be the first safe opened while people have been asleep in the next room. Leah, don't make any mistake. Sammy's good, and this is the only way to handle the situation. You understand, don't you?'

'Oh, yes,' she said. The strange, electric calmness remained in her voice. It puzzled Rollison, and seemed to puzzle the man named Jim. 'And Leo is – *dead.*'

'Listen, Leah.' The man's voice was cracked with anxiety. 'Don't act that way, I don't like it. Leo lost his head over this Riordon job. That stuff has become an obsession, it's all he could think about. He was taking big risks with it, I knew that all along, so did you. Understand, Leah – he wasn't himself, so it went wrong. As if you didn't know. Leah, can you hear me? Are you there?'

'Yes, I'm listening,' she said heavily.

'If Leo had been caught, it would have been all up with us all. Maybe Nevett realized that, and he didn't have any love for Leo. Maybe it was the best way out for all of us, as Leo was losing his grip. Get those papers out of the safe, that's all. Nevett won't squeal, you know that. He may be able to switch this on to Rollison, may get clear. But open that door as soon as Sammy Gilbert comes.'

'All right,' she said. 'All right,' and hung up.

There was plenty of time; at least, sufficient time. He could even give Sammy Gilbert a welcome.

He was within two yards of her when she moved round.

All colour had been drained from her face, the only colour left was in her eyes, and they blazed like blue flames. The rest of her was dead, but her eyes lived. It was as if she had been to hell and had come back, knowing what hell was like.

Rollison fought against the fascination of the dead face with the living eyes.

He didn't speak.

She moved her right hand to her throat and clutched it.

She opened her mouth wider.

'He's – dead,' she said, and the words were like a sigh from a heart that was smashed. 'Leo is dead.'

Rollison forced the unseen hand of paralysis away from him, moistened his lips, and then said:

'Well? Isn't that what you wanted?'

'*Wanted*. You don't understand, he's *dead*.'

It didn't make sense; but he could see the truth, showing clearly now. She had both hate and love for Leo Woolf, and of them, love was stronger. The passion of her emotion explained why he could do what he wanted with her, humiliate and cheat and be unfaithful, and yet be sure that she would do whatever he wanted, and would always be waiting. Rollison knew that as surely as he was standing there. There were times when hatred spilled out, when she wanted to hurt; times almost of madness.

She had talked of killing Woolf.

She had felt, at that moment, that she wanted him dead; she had behaved as she might have done in the middle of a stormy quarrel, flinging hateful, bitter words at him, meaning them in the heat of rage.

But now he was dead, it was as if part of herself had died.

Rollison said gently, 'Leah, listen to me. This won't—'

She raised her hands.

'You did it. You caught him, robbed him, made him helpless, so you did it. You killed him as surely as if you'd fired at him. You. I'll see you hang for it, I'll see you hang.'

XIX

SAMMY

'ALL right, my lovely,' said Rollison, and moved towards her. She didn't back away. 'You'll see me hanged.'

'You killed him, you—'

He struck her beneath the chin, a sharp jab which put her out; the kindest and the quickest way. He supported her as she fell, and carried her to the couch. Then he swung round to the telephone, and dialled the number of the Lumley Street flat.

'Hallo, who's that?' greeted Iris Cartwright.

'Your most devoted admirer, who is wondering why the blazes you—'

'Richard, be quiet! I slipped out the back way and managed to speak to Lady Gloria again. I've a big car, I hired it under a false name. It's parked in a mews near Lumley Street.'

'Iris, you're perfect. Will you bring the car to Mayrick Court, Mayfair, very quickly? It had better wait in the side street nearby – Peel Street. Near the corner of Williton Street.'

'I'll come right away,' Iris promised.

There was Leah Woolf to worry about, and the unknown man named Jim. There would be no reasoning with the woman and little hope of persuasion. He went and examined her. She would be unconscious for five minutes or more, but not long enough. He tied her wrists again, and pushed her own small handkerchief

into her mouth, to make a gag. He turned away
quickly, picked up the sealed envelope and put it in his
pocket. The flat bell rang.

'Hallo, Sam,' he said softly.

The bookcase door was closed, and the doors to the
hall were locked, so there wasn't much that the maid
could do about it if she heard the bell. He went into
the hall, briskly, as the bell rang again. He opened the
door, and a small man whom he had occasionally seen
in the East End, and who certainly knew him, stood
on the threshold.

He moved forward. 'I've bin told to—'

'Welcome, Sam,' said Rollison, warmly.

He gripped the man's shoulder and drew him in,
closed the door quietly, and beamed down at him.
Sammy Gilbert, five feet four in his socks, was a thin
wraith of a man, a brilliant cat-burglar, and an expert
safe-breaker. He stared up from a monkey-like face
and a pair of incredulous brown eyes.

'The – the Torf!' he gasped.

'That's right, Sammy. Come here to do a job for a
friend, haven't you?'

Sammy goggled.

'And don't get any foolish notion that because there's
a call out for me, you can get away with anything,' said
Rollison. 'Who sent you?'

Sammy gulped.

'I dunno 'is nime, 'e—'

'Sammy,' said Rollison reprovingly. He gripped the
little man's scraggy neck; and pressed. Sammy flinched.
'Remember, you can get yourself a lot of trouble. Think
back to the third of June, and your night out and the
Beesley job.'

'I never! I never did that, I—'

'You did, Sammy, and all your friends know it, so do a lot of mine. I haven't squealed on anyone yet, and in your way you're a pleasant little man. Too nice to work for this job. Who sent you tonight?'

Sammy gave up without a real fight.

'Jim Rowse,' he said.

*   *   *

The surname hit Rollison like a physical blow; Jim *Rowse*. He had a mental picture of freckle-faced Reginald of the wild temper. It faded quickly, but not before Sammy had noticed something amiss, and began to protest:

'That's 'oo it was, I swear—'

'And I believe you, Sammy.' Rollison took the black address book from his pocket, and skimmed the pages. James R. Rowse was entered as living at 15 Niel Street, Hampstead; and had a telephone number. 'Yes, I believe you. How long have you worked for him?'

'It's the first job, 'e said it was a pushover, just open a can for a lady.'

'Someone else did it for her. Sammy, how long do you think you'd get for the Beesley job?'

Sammy gulped.

'Now, Mr. Ar, you wouldn't—'

'I have to save my neck, Sammy. Remember it. We're going to take the lady out for a walk. A car will be round the corner in a few minutes, and when we get her inside, you can go. Clean as a whistle, without a stain on your character, and I'll forget all about the third of June.'

Sammy said, 'You never croaked 'er!'

He looked dumbfounded.

'Not yet, Sammy.'

Rollison led the way into the study. Leah Woolf's eyes were open, but she didn't try to move. Rollison glanced at his watch. A car sounded not far off, and stopped nearby; Iris had been quick. It was half past two; there was no sign of the police.

* * *

At Scotland Yard a man was saying into a transmitter:

>'*Calling all cars in AZ Division. Go to Williton Street. Calling all cars in AZ Division. Go to . . .*'

* * *

'There's a night porter, I slipped 'im,' Sammy said hoarsely.

'You can deal with one night porter, Sammy, can't you?'

'Mr. Ar, you're wanted on a murder rap. If I get caught 'elpin' yer—'

'I'll forget the third of June and tell the simple truth, Sammy – that you were forced into it to-night. At the point of a gun, my son.' He flipped his gun out of his pocket and tossed it into the air. 'See?'

Sammy gulped again.

'Okay.'

He went out.

Rollison lifted the woman from her chair and hoisted her over his shoulder; she was heavy, it wouldn't be easy to get her down the stairs; the lift would help. He carried her into the hall, and she didn't protest, didn't kick or struggle. By the time he reached the lift, he was breathing hard. He rested her against the wall and pressed the button, the lift clicked into action at once. As it came up, he opened the doors and helped the woman in.

She made no effort to struggle.

The lift whined down, and stopped.

Rollison opened the doors, and saw Sammy Gilbert at the front door. Rollison hoisted the woman up again, and she muttered something; the handkerchief prevented him from hearing it, but he thought he caught the word 'walk'.

He hurried to the front door.

Sammy said, 'There's a car.'

Headlights were shining from some way off, and glistened on windows. Another car came from a different direction, and the engines of both had an ominous high-pitched whine.

'The cops!'

Rollison said, 'All right, get to the corner.'

He started to run; he was almost beaten, but managed just a jogging step; Leah Woolf bounced up and down on his shoulder. His side hurt. The car was drawing rapidly nearer, but not from the corner where his own car should be. He gritted his teeth and ran on. He turned the corner as the car pulled up behind him, and a man shouted.

Another car was coming along this street, headlights blazing.

Iris sat at the wheel of a big limousine. Sammy had the door open, and had his hands raised, almost in an attitude of prayer. Rollison bundled Leah Woolf into the back, climbed in after her, and saw Sammy get in next to the girl. The nearer car was coming round the corner now, the other was only fifty yards away.

She switched on her headlights and seemed to drive straight at the approaching car. Sammy squealed. Leah Woolf sat rigid, staring at the oncoming headlights.

Iris swung the wheel.

She probably didn't know herself how she managed it, but she swerved on to the pavement between lamp-posts and reached the road beyond the police car – and then her foot went down hard. The engine roared. There was a crash behind them. Rollison looked out of the window, and saw two cars, one broadside across the road.

*   *   *

'You get along, I'll take the car away,' Iris said.

She had stopped fifty yards away from Lumley Street. Sammy was next to her.

'I'm coming wiv you!'

'Dump him somewhere,' Rollison said. 'Thanks, Sammy.'

'Can I do anything else?' asked Iris.

'Be near Bottle Mews, for a bit, will you? You can park a car there all night, and watch from a doorway. Wait as long as you feel you can.' He spoke very quietly. 'All right,' she said. He smiled at her in the light of a street-lamp, and pulled Leah Woolf towards him. She came without a protest, and when he helped her to stand up, she started to walk. He hurried, with an arm on hers, into Lumley Street. He unlocked the front door and led her up. He reached his own flat, and took out his keys – and the door opened.

Jolly said, 'Good evening, sir.'

*   *   *

'Hallo, Jolly,' said Rollison. 'We've a guest. Show Mrs. Woolf to the rest-room, will you? Remember how rattlesnakes behave, too.'

'Good evening, madam,' said Jolly. His expression didn't change when he saw her bound wrists and the handkerchief poking from her lips. He took her arm, and she went with him obediently. He took her into the bedroom, and closed the door.

He was in there with her for three or four minutes.

Rollison caught a glimpse of his own face in an over-mantel mirror. He hadn't any colour. He was still rushing away from patrol cars. He forced a laugh, went to the corner table and poured himself a stiff whisky. Then he lit a cigarette and went back to the mantel-piece, standing with his back to it. A dozen pictures flitted across the mirror of his mind. He pushed them away, took off his coat and pulled up his shirt and singlet. Both were bloodstained.

Jolly came in as he was peering at the patch of blood.

'Straighten up, sir, will you?' Jolly looked, and dabbed with a handkerchief; the cut was perhaps a quarter of an inch deep.

'I brought some first-aid equipment,' Jolly said. 'We'll soon have that patched up, and you can rest.'

He was ten minutes over the patching up; when he had finished the wound wasn't painful at all, and was well plastered and padded.

'Thanks. What have you done with the rattlesnake?' Rollison asked.

'I have made her rather more comfortable, sir, but replaced the handkerchief with a small roll of cotton wool.'

Jolly glanced down at his hand, reflectively; and Rollison saw blood.

'So she bit.'

'A mere trifle, sir.'

'Sorry. Jolly, ought you to be here?'

'I can imagine nowhere else I should be, sir.'

'No police behind you?'

'I was able to evade them, sir, and made quite sure before I came here.'

'Good. I have not had a nice time. I have been murdering more people. With air-guns and things. You'll have to take me in hand, Jolly.'

'I'll do my best, sir. May I be permitted to say that you look really tired?'

'I feel like a fox at the end of the third day's hunt.'

Jolly moved towards him, brown eyes searching, lined face anxious. They stood looking at each other for several seconds, before Jolly relaxed, and moved back – and forced a smile.

'You must be *very* tired, sir, or you wouldn't take a gloomy view.'

'Call it reaction. I'm not tired. I have to see a Mr. James Rowse tonight. He lives at 15 Niel Street, Hampstead, and he was awake less than an hour ago. He'll almost certainly be awake now. He was in the confidence of Mr. Leo Woolf. Mr. Woolf had a knife – *our* knife, Jolly – with our finger-prints on, if you see what I mean. Our knife cut Mr. Keller's throat as Miss Lane's spanner cracked his skull.'

'Do we know Mr. Woolf, sir?'

Rollison finished his whisky, and stubbed out his cigarette.

'I feel almost new again. Don't go on holiday for so

long next time. Yes, we know him. He framed Marion-Liz and framed me. He was certainly after the Riordon collection. Alive, I think he might have been a useful witness, I'd have taken a chance and handed him over to Grice. But he wouldn't stay alive.'

'I see,' said Jolly, mildly.

'I brought his wife here, instead. She knows a lot, not everything. She also works with our Mr. James Rowse, who may or may not be a brother of Reginald. I wonder if Reginald lives at Hampstead.'

'No, sir, in Earls Court. For the night, he has accommodation at Cannon Row, after assaulting Mr. Grice.'

'Oh. Well, look after Mrs. Woolf, won't you? Yes, I know I'd handle it better if I waited until morning, but I'd hate to try to get that knife back from Cannon Row or Brixton Jail. Oh, if I shouldn't come back, and you have to try to bail me out, this might come in handy.' He gave Jolly the address-book and the envelope. 'Go through the women, and find out which of them might be taken for Marion-Elizabeth Lane by people who don't know her well.'

Jolly looked his agony.

'Having anyone else here?' Rollison asked.

'Skinner will be back in a few minutes, sir.'

'Good.'

Rollison nodded, smiled, and went out.

XX

DAWN

I⊤ was four o'clock.

The eastern sky was faintly light. London's sparrows, starlings, and pigeons were stirring noisily. The stars were fading, even in the west and above his head. The air was clear and invigorating, with a promise of a fine, cool day to come; the thunder had broken the pressure.

Rollison walked quickly towards Oxford Street, choosing narrow alleys where he could, hardly troubled by the pain at his waist.

He had Leah Woolf, on the credit side. What of the debit?

The knife might be anywhere; might possibly have been in the flat above Marion-Liz. That wasn't likely, Jim Rowse probably had it.

Rowse—

He refused to be side-tracked; he was examining the debit balance, and it was much too heavy. He needn't weigh up Marion-Liz's side again, he had plenty to think of with his own. The attack on Grice; the attack on the policeman; the burglaries.

There remained the knife; above everything, his knife, so neatly stolen from Devon and used with such great cunning. Of course it had his prints on it; and of course the frame-up had been worked to include him – a perfect job.

Woolf's?

Or Jim Rowse's?

Possibly even Nevett's; the man had a quick mind, as he'd proved that night. His story that Rollison shot Woolf wouldn't stand up against Reginald Rowse's evidence and the girl's. Well, it shouldn't; but the girl's evidence might mean little when prosecuting counsel had finished with her, and Reginald Rowse *might* be persuaded to withdraw his statement if the other Rowse had any influence with him. Were they brothers?

He turned a corner.

Two policemen, constable and sergeant, were conferring a little way along. He felt their gaze on him as he hurried past the end of the street. He heard a car, the engine snorting, but didn't glance round.

It muffled the sound of policemen's feet; he couldn't judge whether he was being followed. He wanted to run to the nearest side street, and wouldn't let himself. He wanted to glance round, as the car snorted nearer, but forced himself to look straight ahead. He thought he heard a new sound; as of brakes going on sharply. Tires screeched – not loudly, but with noise enough to send his nerves screaming, to make him clench his hands and grit his teeth.

A red-nosed car edged past him, colour bright even in the faint dawn light, and a girl whispered:

'Richard!'

He turned, stung. Iris sat at the wheel of her little two-seater, with the door beside her open, eagerness in her eyes. He could have kissed her. He sprang into the car, and the door slammed. He looked round, and there was no sign of the two policemen. He squeezed her hand.

'Don't, while I'm driving.'

He laughed; he couldn't stop laughing.

'I don't know what's happened to you,' said Iris impatiently, 'but I don't think it's a laughing matter. *I'm* taking big risks to help you. I was waiting at the Mews, and thought I recognized you.'

'My sweet, you're more wonderful even than I knew. Turn right, will you?'

She turned right.

'Do you know the way to Hampstead?'

'Of course I do.'

'Good,' said Rollison.

She trod on the accelerator, glanced at him, and yet held her peace; she was a wonderful woman.

'Why are we going to Hampstead?' Iris asked at last.

'A man lives there who has something belonging to me. I hope.'

'What is it?'

'Must we go into details?'

'Well, I think you owe me that,' said Iris, and looked stormily ahead of her. An early morning cyclist turned out of a side street, and she had to swing out to avoid him. 'The fool!'

'This man had a knife of mine, it helped to kill Keller. It has my prints on it. So I'm not going for a pleasant chat.'

She shot him a startled glance; she was as impulsive and as freshly naïve as a child, for all her courage and loyalty.

'Do the police know?'

'I don't think so – yet. I'd be much happier if I could wipe the blood off it, and clear the finger-prints away.'

'Yes, so would I,' said Iris. 'Richard, how on earth did you come to get mixed up with devils like these?'

'It just happens that way.'

There was a long, straight stretch of road, and no traffic, and she took her eyes off the road in front to look at him steadily. As he stared back, he saw her lips soften and her eyes full of something not far from sympathy, and she said softly:

'You're scared, aren't you?'

He would not have admitted it to another woman in the world, except perhaps Old Glory.

'Yes,' he said.

'I'll get you to Hampstead,' she said. 'We shan't be long. But – have you thought that the police might be there first?'

He didn't answer.

'Have you, Richard?'

'Yes, my sweet, I've thought of that.'

She was doing fifty miles an hour in a thirty-mile-limit district, and from the look of her face, she would gladly have stepped up the speed to eighty or ninety.

*　　　*　　　*

The morning light was keen and searching by the time they reached Hampstead Heath. The Heath itself was deserted, and the freshness of the new day gave the leaves of trees and bushes a new glory. The grass, damp from the overnight rain, had a silvery sheen upon its green. The roads were dry. Two motorists passed them, and they passed several cyclists, one a policeman moving steadily, as if he would bore his way through all the criminals of London. Doubtless he was thinking that the dark hours for crime were past.

Rollison kept his face averted as Iris drove past the man.

Niel Street, near the common, was a wide thorough-fare, tree-lined, with massive houses on either side, all standing in their own grounds; and the grounds of all were bright with flowers of every colour, lawns were trim and neat. Some of the houses were old and ugly with the Victorian redness of brick and unexpectedness of turrets; many were new, and smaller.

Number 15 was one of these.

It stood back from the road, a pleasant and imposing residence, with a green-tiled roof, white walls, wide steps leading to a loggia and the front door – which was in fact at the side – facing south. Cupressus-trees spiked along the front wall, so that they could catch only glimpses of the place as they passed. A drive with a wide carriageway, near the house itself, glowed yellow in the first glint of the sun. This was new and prosperous.

Iris slackened her pace so that Rollison could see as much as possible – including the small, new car which stood in the drive. The gateway was half-way along the street, and she drove as far as the corner.

'No police, anyhow,' she said with relief.

'They keep giving us time.'

'Where do you want me to wait?'

She had pulled up at the side of the road, and was looking at him full face, eyes hopeful and eager.

He rested a hand on hers.

'I don't want you to wait, my sweet. I want you to go home and stay there.'

'You're talking out of the back of your neck!'

'All right, then! Go to Aunt Gloria, and keep her company. She'll be needing company, she has the oddest affection for her prodigal nephew. Tell her all's well, so far.'

161

'She wouldn't believe me, and anyhow, I'm staying here.'

'For the police to find, if they get here in time.' Rollison chuckled. 'Iris, if taking risks with you would really help, I'd take them, because you'd want me to. But that wouldn't help. This is the end of the hunt. Either I'm to be lucky or things really go wrong. I expect to find what I want here, and if I do, I can lift the telephone and send for the police. That'll be that. If I don't—'

'You'll need to get away somewhere, in a hurry.'

'If I don't, I'll have shot my bolt. No, this isn't because I want to get you out of danger, it's simple fact. And it's a job I can only do on my own.'

She didn't answer.

'I started it alone, and I'll see it through alone,' went on Rollison. 'Don't look obstinate, and don't be glum. Go back and help Jolly. He knows where I am.'

She shrugged.

'All right,' she said. 'I'll go. But I'll walk to the nearest tube, and leave the car here. Will it be all right here?'

'It's a good thought. The police might recognize it.'

'You *may* need it.'

'All right,' Rollison said. 'You do as you like.'

She got out, and he followed her. No one watched as they stood face to face, the girl a few inches shorter than Rollison. In the morning light she was as wholesome and lovely as at any time of night or day. Suddenly, she took his hands and kissed him, on the cheek – and then she turned and ran; actually ran.

Rollison watched her out of sight.

Then he rasped his fingers over the stubble of his face, and walked quickly towards Number 15.

The police weren't here; Rollison didn't seriously think they were being cagey, and watching from under cover; but he glanced into several of the big gardens near Number 15, from which the grounds could be seen. No one lurked there. The small car, a Morris, still stood outside the front door, and now the sun glistened on its black roof and sides and scintillated from the chromium of headlamps and fittings.

Rollison opened the gate and went into the grounds.

By night, he might have been able to approach unobserved; that was impossible now, the garden was fairly new and open, the only cover was the cupressus-trees, behind him. The drive sloped upwards. He walked briskly, making no attempt to hurry, and went towards the front door. He watched the broad bay windows, but no one moved near them, he saw nothing to suggest that he was being observed.

He reached the loggia and the front door. The floor was polished red, but sand from the drive had been washed and blown on to it by the storm, small pieces of gravel grated under his feet.

It was an ordinary Yale lock.

He took out a strip of mica.

The door opened, and a man stood there, smiling at him sardonically; a red-headed man – an older version of Reginald Rowse.

XXI

OFFER

'Good morning,' said Rollison pleasantly.

'So you've made it,' said Rowse. 'I expected you.'

'Blessed is he who gets what he expects,' said Rollison. 'I hope you're expecting plenty.' His right hand was in his pocket; so was Rowse's. 'May I come in?'

'I should hate to let you go,' said Rowse.

He was not only ten years or so older than Reginald, but he was taller and more powerful – not unlike Woolf, in a way, with a round face and a fair skin and hair which was not so decided a red as Reginald's. His eyes were greeny-grey, quite nice eyes. He had a square chin, and a nose which was only slightly snub.

He stood aside.

Rollison stepped in.

Men might close in on him from either side; Rowse certainly wouldn't be alone. No one else moved in the spacious hall, and Rowse closed the door softly. He smiled with his lips compressed as Rollison glanced at several doorways, the wide staircase, and in all the corners.

'We'll go in here,' said Rowse.

He waited for Rollison to go ahead, while he pointed at a room with a partly open door. Rollison went forward, casually – then kicked the door open and stepped in swiftly. He saw a man, standing in a corner, ducking below the top of a screen.

He grinned.

'Playing hide and seek so early in the morning? What a constitution.'

'All right, Steve, you can show yourself,' Rowse said.

There was an edge to his voice, which was otherwise pleasant enough. Woolf had looked a rogue, Rowse didn't.

The man called Steve straightened up, his face red with embarrassment. He was small, and he didn't appear to have much intelligence – a dumb type who came forward and rubbed the barrel of a gun with his left hand, as if he wanted to hide it and knew that would be impossible. He had a long, sorrowful face and not much hair.

'Make yourself comfortable,' said Rollison. 'Where's the lady, Rowse?'

'Which one?'

'Lizzie's near double.'

Rowse shrugged.

'You needn't worry about her, she was paid for the job, and that's that. She wouldn't come forward if the police searched for a year. Don't kid yourself.'

'Even I can hope.'

'You can't hope much,' said Rowse, and there was a heavier note in his voice, a hint of menace which might have been borrowed from Woolf. 'Go and sit down. Steve, go and make some tea – or would you rather have coffee, Rollison?'

'My dear chap, what hospitality! Tea. Thanks.'

'Micky, you didn't ought—' began Steve.

'I can handle Rollison,' Rowse said, and Steve went out.

'Micky Rowse,' murmured Rollison. 'I prefer it to

Jim, it sounds like something out of Walt Disney.'

He watched Steve sidle out of the door, and knew that Rowse was watching him closely. He went to an easy-chair, which was wide and capacious, and sat down; he didn't take his hand from his pocket or from his gun. He leaned forward and helped himself to a cigarette and lit it from a table-lighter.

'Well, what's to do?'

'How much did you take from Woolf's place?'

'Everything that matters.'

Rowse said, 'I wish I could be sure, but I think you took plenty. If you hadn't, the police would have been here by now. I took a chance that you'd empty the safe before you left.'

'That puts you in my debt,' said Rollison.

'Where's the stuff you took?'

'Nicely cared for, thank you.'

'Got it with you?'

'Search me.'

'I will soon,' said Rowse. 'Did it include an address-book and a sealed envelope?'

Rollison stretched out his legs and laughed, ignoring the question.

'Funny how things work out, isn't it? You've a knife with my dabs on, and I've some papers which will probably send you down for ten years and might get you hanged. We ought to do a deal.'

'And that's why you came?'

'Isn't it why you expected me?'

Rowse laughed softly.

'Yes, I suppose it is.'

He walked across to the window and stood with his back to it. There were faint sounds from somewhere

else in the house. Rollison doubted if these two men
were the only ones here; there were bound to be others.
He felt relaxed, and was able to look it. This was the
last battle, there would be no more running, no more
probing – he'd staked everything, and he thought the
odds were even. He didn't ask for more.

Rowse said, 'So you'll exchange the stuff you took
from Woolf's place for the knife.'

'Plus.'

'Plus what?'

'A statement, about who killed Keller, how Liz and
I were framed, when you stole my knife, what this is all
about. Plus.'

'Plus what else?'

'Keller's killer.'

'Oh, no,' said Rowse. 'You haven't a chance to get
him. You won't get his name, either. In fact, I don't
think you're going to get much of anything, Mr.
Ruddy Toff. Where's Leah Woolf?'

'Missing her already?'

'Where is she?'

'Comfortable, dumb, and at my disposal. Mine and
my friends. I thought perhaps you'd forgotten that
Leah is an important witness, too.'

'You'd never dare let the police get her,' said Rowse.

'Why not?'

'I know Leah. I could tell what she was like on the
telephone. She's as nearly crazy as anything on two
legs. She could love and hate Leo in the same breath.
She was always breathing fire about him, but if anyone
else said a word against him or did him any harm, she
would lose her head. I know Leah. She'll blame you for
his death, and she'll swear black's white if it'll send

167

you to the gallows. Don't count Leah among your trumps, Rollison.'

Steve came in, with tea, and started to pour out.

'I'll do that,' said Rowse. 'Scram.'

Steve protested, mutely, and went out again. Rowse poured tea, pushed a cup towards Rollison, picked up his own, and went back to the window; and Rollison chuckled.

'What's funny?'

'You and me and tea,' said Rollison. 'Things like this ought to go with raw Scotch.'

'I don't drink,' said Rowse. 'That makes sure I keep my wits about me all the time. I don't drink and I don't smoke, and—'

'All the virtues!' Rollison mocked.

'Enough. And I know exactly what I want, and always get it. I want the papers you stole from Woolf's safe. I want Leah Woolf. And when I've got them, you can have the knife.'

Rollison sipped his tea.

'Or else,' said Rowse, ominously.

'Ah, the snag.' Rollison looked at him with narrowed eyes. 'In fact, there are several snags. I don't trust you, Reginald's brother.'

'You can leave Reggie out of this.'

'I wish I thought so. What I can't be sure is where he comes in.' So the Rowses were brothers; as if that mattered at all now. 'I don't trust you. I'd want my hands on that knife and the full story, before I passed anything over. Shall we have a look at the knife?'

Rowse touched his coat.

Rollison said, 'Well, well, so you have it in your pocket!'

'That's right. And if I get trouble from you, I'll knock you out, put it in *your* pocket, and call the police. They'd enjoy finding that.'

'They'd enjoy finding the papers which name you.'

Rowse said, 'Listen, Rollison, there are some things you have to get straight. I might be caught by the police, and get a long stretch. That's always been on the cards, don't make any mistake about it. But they can't get me for murder – and they can get you. Don't make any mistake about that, either. I'll back my chances against yours, but I'd rather keep clear of trouble. That's why I'll give you a break. After I've got the papers and Leah, you can have the knife.'

He put his hand to his pocket.

Rollison sat, tensed, ready to spring.

Rowse called, 'Steve!' and immediately the man appeared in the doorway. He covered Rollison with his gun, as Rowse took out a flat cardboard box which would just fit into a large pocket. The box was tied round with string. As he handled it, he held out one hand, palm upwards. There were strips of adhesive tape over the tips of his fingers, so he would make no fresh prints.

He took the lid off the box, and then took out a knife – wrapped in tissue paper. He pulled the paper off. It was Rollison's, beyond shadow of doubt. In the blade and also on the hilt were brown stains; and there was little doubt that they were of human blood: Harry Keller's.

'If the police get you and this, you've had it,' said Rowse. 'Just as surely as Lizzie Lane's had it, too.'

'I was coming to Marion-Liz,' said Rollison, softly.

'You can forget her.'

Rollison made no answer.

'You can forget her,' repeated Rowse. 'If you get this knife back, you can call yourself Lucky. Liz will hang. You'll just withdraw your story that you were with her, leave that couple of hours in her life blank. Liz is finished, but for her Leo wouldn't have died. I knew he was getting too reckless because of the Riordon job. Now I liked Leo. And I don't like Liz.'

Rollison shrugged.

'So get it straight. You might squeeze out yourself, and the knife would help you. Take a good look at it. With that as an exhibit, the Public Prosecutor could send you to the gallows. Without it, you'd squeeze out. Forget Liz – just remember where those papers are and where Leah is, and fix it so that I get them both. I want them soon. Tell me how you're going to do it, too.'

Rollison said, 'We've a lot to discuss, yet. I don't like the terms.'

'Don't you?' asked Rowse softly, and he raised his voice again. 'Tommy!'

Another man appeared, who must have been waiting outside for this signal. He was hefty, and had a face which would have put Bill Ebbutt's to shame. There was a vicious glint in small, dark eyes, and he had once had a nasty wound in his face, which gave him a perpetual leer. He came forward heavily – but went behind Rollison.

'Where can I get Leah and those papers, Rollison?' Rowse's voice was soft again.

Rollison relaxed, and put down his empty cup.

'Okay, Tommy,' said Rowse.

A blow on the side of the head made Rollison's ears

ring. Another, on the other side, seemed to split his head in two. Then great hands fastened round his neck and began to choke him. There wasn't a thing he could do. The pressure of those powerful fingers was like death itself. Rollison felt his head whirling, and the room went dark. There was a tight band round his chest, he heaved in the terrible effort to breathe, but couldn't draw a breath. The darkness became blackness, and he seemed to lose the power of thought.

The pressure relaxed.

It seemed an age before he saw Rowse clearly – and even then the man seemed to be moving up and down and round and about. The room was unsteady, and two great lumps seemed to press against Rollison's wind-pipe.

Rowse said: 'Like it? That's just a beginning Rollison. Tommy will do what I tell him. He's had a lot of experience in making people uncomfortable. Where's Leah? Where are those papers?'

Tommy rapped hard knuckles against Rollison's temples.

'Painful?' asked Rowse. 'Perhaps you'd rather have the police, and that knife in your pocket. Look.' He held the knife close to Rollison's eyes, point forward; the dulled blade was sharp, there was only a little of the bright steel still untouched by blood. 'Look! You can have it back, if you'll tell me where Leah and those papers are. If not—'

He stabbed forward with it.

The point seemed to enter Rollison's eyes. There was a spasm of dreadful pain – but it wasn't physical, the knife didn't touch the eye.

Rowse drew back.

'He won't last long,' he said confidently. 'He hasn't been used to real rough stuff. Ease off for a few minutes, Tommy.'

The man stood back.

'Take a rest and do some serious thinking,' said Rowse. 'And remember you wouldn't have a chance in hell if you hadn't taken Leah and the papers. Just talk.'

If he talked, what? Death? Or a mocking laugh and a blow which would knock him out, the knife in his pocket, and the police on the way? That was the probable end; there would be no honour in Rowse's promise. The man knew exactly what he wanted, and would stop at nothing to get it. The thoughts passed laboriously through Rollison's mind; he was almost past thinking.

Then he heard a cry.

'Micky!'

It was a woman's voice. He heard running footsteps down the stairs, and the call came again.

'Micky, look out of the window!'

A girl swung into the room. She was young and attractive, and she might have been taken for Marion-Liz. She had the same colouring, the same kind of figure. Rollison's gaze was hazy, he couldn't really see her clearly. He knew she hadn't Marion-Liz's ravishing beauty, but she would do. She rushed across the room to Rowse, as he turned towards the window and looked out.

He stood rigid.

Rollison's thought, 'Police?' And it hardly seemed to matter.

Rowse swung round – and laughed. Laughed on a loud and triumphant note, making Steve grin broadly.

The girl hung on to Rowse's arm, he put an arm round her shoulders and hugged her.

He moved in front of Rollison.

'You make a lot of mistakes, don't you?' he said. 'Leah's coming up the drive. Steve! Go and open the door.'

XXII

LAST MISTAKE

STEVE hurried out of the room. Rowse laughed again, slid his arm round the girl's waist, and they went towards the door. If Leah had escaped—

Leah *had* escaped.

She probably had the papers with her. Jolly had failed, no one could blame Jolly, but at this crucial stage he'd failed. Rollison leaned back – and caught sight of Tommy, staring towards the door. He had a fore-shortened view of Tommy's massive chin and bulging nostrils. His neck still hurt and his breathing was painful, but Tommy's attention was on the door, and the others were going out into the hall.

Rollison stretched up his arms.

Tommy saw that, and started – and Rollison got his fingers round Tommy's thick throat, and squeezed. Even Tommy's strength of grip couldn't have held on more tightly.

'Leah!' cried Rowse, from the hall.

'Darling!' crowed the girl.

Tommy made a choking noise and smashed at Rollison's head. The blows hurt, but didn't make him relax his grip. He pressed into the wind-pipe, could feel Tommy's heaving chest, felt also the slackening power of the blows.

Tommy went limp.

Rollison squeezed him again, for safety's sake, and

let him go. He fell, slackly, slid down by the back of the chair and lay in a heap on the floor. Rollison got up slowly, and his head reeled. He wasn't out of this wood yet, but he could see the path. They'd made a big mistake, a fatal one; they'd been so sure of themselves that they hadn't searched him.

He took out his gun, and stepped towards a corner, near the door.

The girl was saying, 'Leah, it's wonderful, we thought you were a prisoner. Rollison—'

'Micky, we're going to get Rollison,' Leah Woolf said. Her voice was rich and deep, with all the attractiveness Rollison had first noticed when she had spoken just behind him. 'I won't rest until—'

'We've got him!' the girl cried.

Leah said, '*No!*'

'Yes, he came here,' said Rowse with a laugh in his voice, triumph was oozing out of him. 'He took a chance, we were just using a little persuasion.' They were much nearer the door, now, would be in at any moment. 'Leah – did you get the papers?'

She said, 'Everything, yes.'

'Wonderful!'

'But how did you do it?' cried the girl who was like Marion-Liz.

'He left two men to look after me,' said Leah. 'One of them left. And you can thank your friend Sammy Gilbert.'

Sammy; oh, Sammy!

'He decided that it was safer to back you than Rollison. He was at our flat. Rollison made him help him, but Sammy knew where he'd come. He watched, saw Rollison's servant leave, and then came and broke

175

into Rollison's hide-out. The other man wasn't expecting trouble, it was soon over.'

Relief showed in her voice, she was gloating.

She stepped into the room, looking at the girl, who was by her side.

'I found the address-book and the papers in a drawer, just had to open the drawer to get them,' said Leah, and laughed; and then her voice changed. 'But he killed Leo, we've got to make sure that Rollison hangs.'

'He would have hanged anyhow,' Rowse said. 'I dangled the knife in front of his nose, carrots to a donkey. Hear that, Rollison?'

Rollison heard him break off as they came into the room, and saw the woman stare towards the empty chair.

Rollison said mildly, 'Anyone like to get hurt?'

Rowse spun round, his hand moving towards his pocket.

'I shouldn't,' said Rollison, and fired. He didn't try to miss Rowse's gun-hand. Blood leapt on to the man's fingers before the hand touched his pocket. The women stood as if transfixed, as the shot roared out. Rollison moved like a flash, pulling Leah farther into the room. She stumbled into the girl, and they fell against the wall, together. Rowse was backing into the hall, Steve was between him and the front door – and Steve had the gun.

He fired.

Rollison felt the bullet tug at his coat as he squeezed the trigger; and his aim was better than the startled Steve's. Steve gasped and staggered back, but still held his gun. Rollison rushed at him, and knocked the gun out of his hand. It wouldn't have mattered. Steve had a wound in his chest and a strange, scared look in his eyes. His knees bent beneath him, and he fell forward.

Rowse's eyes were rounded with the same fear.

'Having a nice time?' Rollison asked. 'Join the ladies, Jim-Micky Rowse, we're going to have some fun.'

He pushed the man back towards the room. He went in cautiously, but neither of the women appeared to have a gun, they stood by a table, limp, dumbfounded. Rollison pushed Rowse towards them, and thrust his fingers through his hair – and hoped they didn't know how weak he felt at the knees.

'And here we are together,' he said foolishly. 'Leah with the papers, too, a nice present for the police.'

Rowse muttered, 'Police? You wouldn't—'

'Now don't be silly,' said Rollison, and went towards the telephone. 'There's a time and a place for everything, including the police. With all of you huddled together like this, they'd hate to miss the party. One of you might even think of turning Queen's Evidence – the sweet young thing who went to Hexley last Wednesday, perhaps.'

The girl said, 'No, no!'

She had lost all her colour, terror shone in her eyes.

'Yes, yes,' mimicked Rollison. 'Not that you'll stand up to police questioning, my pretty. We can show them everything now, including the knife in your pocket, Micky. Before I telephone them—'

Rowse said, 'Rollison, listen! We can pay you for silence, give us a break. We can pay plenty, we—'

'Oh, not that,' protested Rollison, as if hurt. 'It's a waste of breath.'

He touched the telephone – and heard a car coming along the road. He glanced out of the window, through which he could see the cupressus-trees and the wall and the top of a car, beyond the wall. Police? He didn't lift the receiver. The car was slowing down, and it stopped with a squeal of brakes – and immediately afterwards another car appeared, coming at speed.

The gates were pushed open.

Men streamed in along the drive, and several cut across the lawns. In the front was Bill Ebbutt; and his cronies from the gymnasium were behind him, four in the first group, five in the next, who came from the second car. Then a third car pulled up, and next moment Jolly and Iris appeared, and ran with surprising speed.

Rowse and the girl looked out of the window.

Leah Woolf stared at Rollison. Her eyes were glittering in that now familiar glare, and her teeth showed because her lips were turned back. She was as beautiful as a lioness at bay.

Footsteps sounded clearly on the gravel.

Rollison said, 'Friends of mine.'

But he didn't smile, nothing in the woman's face encouraged a smile. He heard a thud at the door and then the crash of breaking glass; Ebbutt was not standing on ceremony. Another window smashed, and a man climbed through and shouted:

'I'm in!'

Men appeared at the window, and Rowse and the girl backed away.

Leah Woolf didn't speak, but drew herself up and

then flung herself forward, ignoring the gun. Rollison could have shot her, but he didn't. He stepped to one side and she followed; then he saw the knife in her hand. She closed with him, knocking his gun aside; and he'd given her the chance because she was a woman! He felt her breath on his face, struggled to get at the wrist, felt the knife tear through the cloth of his coat, felt the cut in his shoulder.

Then men rushed in.

She was dragged away, gasping for breath – and suddenly began to shout and rave. It took Ebbutt and two others to hold her down in a chair, and all Ebbutt's strength to pull the knife from her fingers. She sat back, snarling; more animal than human.

Ebbutt wheezed, 'You okay, Mr. Ar?' He loomed over Rollison, who was standing upright with difficulty and whose shoulder was throbbing. A great arm went round his waist. 'Take it easy, Mr. Ar. Just lean on me. We'll git you away, Jolly's fixed a car and a n'airyplane.'

Rollison leaned against him.

Jolly and Iris came in, the girl in front.

'Richard! Oh, Richard, thank God you're all right!'

'But we've got to get a move on,' said Ebbutt. 'The rozzers might be rahnd anytime, can't trust the rozzers. I'll carry yer, Mr. Ar, just take it easy.'

Jolly came across hurriedly, his eyes searching for the truth – for hope.

Rollison forced a grin.

'All right, Bill. All right, Jolly. No more running. The knife's in Rowse's pocket, everything the police will want is here – including the pretty who pretended to be Marion-Liz. All over, bar the shouting. There'll be a lot of shouting, but who minds that?'

After a long pause, Jolly said, 'Are you sure, sir?'
'Quite sure,' said Rollison.

*   *   *

The prisoners were taken into another room, and this large, airy room, with its brightness and luxury, was very quiet. Rollison sat in an easy-chair, coat off and shoulder bandaged. Jolly finished the bandaging and stood back. Iris stood by the window, looking towards the street and waiting for the police. Two or three of Ebbutt's men were on guard in the rest of the house, but most of them had gone. Ebbutt himself was watching the prisoners.

'I can't tell you how sorry I am about the mishap at Lumley Street, sir.' Jolly was himself again. 'I left Skinner in charge, because I wanted to make arrangements for an aircraft, I envisaged the possibility that it would be wise for you to leave the country for a short while. I had not calculated on Gilbert's treachery, of course. Miss Cartwright tells me that he left the car a few moments after she drove away from the spot near Lumley Street, and obviously he doubled back and saw where you went. I simply had not allowed for that, and naturally had thought that Skinner would be capable of dealing with any emergency.'

Rollison smiled faintly.

'Does it matter, now?'

'I feel that it does, sir, although not so much as it might have done. When I found what had happened, I rang up Mr. Ebbutt, and came back here with Miss Cartwright, we had a job getting a taxi so early. Are you *quite* sure it is wise to face the police at this juncture, sir?'

'Yes, Jolly.'

'Of course he is,' said Iris, swinging round violently. 'What a daft thing to say, Jolly. I wouldn't be surprised if you don't put him up to half the crazy things he does. And if he gets into trouble for hitting that policeman, it won't do him any harm. No harm at all.' Her lips were trembling. 'It's absolute madness for a man like you to go about risking your life. When are you going to stop?'

'When the bad men stop working,' said Rollison.

'Oh, you fool!'

She swung away from him, and Rollison smiled – and saw an answering smile in Jolly's eyes. Then Iris, changeable as the weather on an April day, swung round from the window.

'They're here!' she cried. 'The police are here.'

*　　*　　*

Two patrol cars arrived first; Grice came half an hour later.

XXIII

OF REGINALD ROWSE AND MARION-LIZ

GRICE came briskly into the room, and Rollison looked first into his eyes and then at his chin. Nothing could hide the bruise on that long jaw. Rollison raised one eyebrow, looking up into the Superintendent's eyes again, and let his lips curve in a smile.

'I won't give no trouble, Guv'nor,' he said, in a fair imitation of Skinner's voice. 'It's a fair cop.'

Grice said, 'You blistering fool.'

'Yes, sir.'

'You deserve to hang.'

'I never killed no one, Mister.'

Grice said savagely, 'You look as if you've had a rough time, and for once I'm glad about that. Perhaps this will bring you to your senses. How long did you leave the Lane girl on Wednesday night?'

'Oh, lor',' said Rollison, ruefully, 'do we have to go into all that again? Bill, I was with her from half past eight until half past two, remember. She didn't go away, and she didn't kill Keller. I don't yet know who did. The girl taken for Marion-Liz is in another room here, and I don't know her name, either. You'll probably find a dress like one of Marion-Liz's, too. Sorry, but you'd like something left for the maws of the Yard, wouldn't you?'

'So you're sticking to that story.'

'Tight as glue. With some evidence.'

Rollison went into some detail, but before he finished, Grice cut him short.

'We can hear all that at the Yard. Middleton!'

Sergeant Middleton came in promptly.

'Richard Rollison,' said Grice in a heavy voice, 'it is my duty to charge you with obstructing the police in the course of their duty, striking a police-officer, which is common assault, and I have to warn you that anything you say may be used in evidence. All right, Sergeant, take him to the Yard. I'll come as soon as I can.'

Iris cried, 'But he didn't do it, you can't—'

'If I were you, Miss Cartwright,' said Grice heavily, 'I should keep quiet until I start to question you. Jolly, you will return to Gresham Terrace and wait there until I send for you. Come on, Rollison.'

'I'll come quietly,' said the Toff humbly.

*　　　*　　　*

He was remanded for eight days; on bail.

At the second hearing, the magistrate fined him twenty-five pounds. The police preferred no other charges. That against Reginald Rowse, for striking Grice, was dropped.

*　　　*　　　*

The trial of Leah Woolf, the elder Rowse, Nevett, and the girl, whose name was Lois Denton, took up five days of the Old Bailey Calendar that autumn. It had more space in all the newspapers than any other case of the year. Much transpired.

The Woolfs had been accomplices of Marion-Liz's father in his crimes, and it was only one of their major crimes. With James Michael Rowse, they had organized robberies, confidence tricks, crime on a large scale; and Leo Woolf had believed that when he got the Riordon collection he could call it a day. It had obsessed him, he'd worked and planned to get at the cache.

He had given evidence for Lane's defence, and so had won the loyalty of Marion-Liz. He had believed that she had the keys to the strong-room where the collection was hidden, and knew where the strong-room was.

She swore that she did not know.

He had given her a few gay weeks, renting a furnished flat for her, and then dropped her. That was normal; and his normal behaviour had worked on his wife's nerves until she had become distraught and neurasthenic, but beneath it all, passionately devoted to him; and he had traded on that. It was an ugly story, but none of the ugliness which came out in court matched that which Rollison had seen at the Woolf's flat or the Hampstead house.

Marion-Liz had called the Woolf *affaire* a closed book, although she was nervous of him, and started to work with Eddie-Harry Keller. All that she had told Rollison about her plans to work with Keller, she said in court, was true; but her bitterness seemed to have gone. Judge and jury could not fail to be favourably impressed. She said she hadn't been sure that Woolf still believed she could get at the Riordon cache. He'd watched and waited his chance, learned of the quarrel with Keller, planned swiftly and struck. He had intended to frame her, by luring her to Hexley; when she didn't go, and he discovered she had gone out with Rollison, he had framed Rollison as well. The independent witness had speeded up the police work, but the gang had framed Liz perfectly.

Nevett had actually killed Keller. Nevett had stolen Rollison's knife. Nevett, later, had killed Woolf because he knew Woolf, if caught, would lead to disaster for him, Rowse, and Leah Woolf; the papers in his safe would have damned them all. Lois Denton had passed for Marion-Liz, and weapons with carefully preserved prints had been used.

Most of the truth came from the Denton girl, who turned Queen's Evidence; much from Marion-Liz; more from the papers taken from Woolf's safe; these damned Woolf's accomplices, and provided evidence on their own which gave the police all they needed; and included the fact that Nevett had actually killed Keller. Liz had once told Woolf, in their palmy days, that if ever she were in trouble, she would go to her friend's flat in Kensington. Woolf had bought out the flat tenant, and put his own man there. She went there – and played into his hands.

One part of Marion-Liz's evidence held Rollison as enthralled as the rest of the court. It was simple and straightforward, and explained much that was mystifying.

When she had parted from Woolf, she had said that she was going to consult Rollison. She couldn't ask the police to help, she'd used Rollison's name to try to frighten Woolf off. That, she said, was why she had gone to Devon, but she'd lacked the courage to make the request. She didn't mention the missing buoy or the quarrel with Keller, she said she'd contemplated a life of crime but not actually started it. The jury might not have been so willing to believe her, but for the story of the burn scars and her insistence that she had no idea where the Riordon collection was or where the keys of the vaults could be found.

She defended Reginald Rowse passionately. She hadn't really run away from him; she had been frightened about the murder, and gone away, making Rowse the excuse. He was just a friend. She didn't believe that Reginald was a criminal. He couldn't help his relations, *he* was as honest as the day. And Reginald, in evidence, said that he had no idea of the life his brother led, although it was true that it was through Jim-Micky that he'd met Marion-Liz and fallen in love.

The Denton girl had made it clear that Micky Rowse had decided that Woolf's obsession might be too dangerous; had been a party to the frame up, and waited for a chance to get rid of Woolf. Nevett earlier had rushed up to London and pushed a letter through Rollison's letter-box, written on paper which Keller had handled; another part of the framing of the Toff.

And Reginald Rowse and Marion-Liz gave eye-witness evidence of the killing of Woolf.

So it ended . . .

Except for Reginald Rowse, Marion-Liz, and the Toff.

*   *   *

Rollison invited the two to the Gresham Terrace flat, a week after the trial. Jolly, lined of face and sorrowful looking, served drinks and went out, but left the door ajar, so that he could hear exactly what was said. It was six o'clock. At half past six, Iris Cartwright and Lady Gloria were due, and Rollison thought that half an hour would be sufficient for his purpose. He stood by the trophy wall where the front page of a newspaper, with his photograph and TOFF HUNTED BY C.I.D., was framed and glazed. He was tall and bronzed and with a gay light in his eyes, showing no signs of what had happened, cuts healed, and bruises long forgotten. He was an amiable host.

Reginald Rowse sat on the arm of a chair, with an arm round Marion-Liz's shoulder. She looked pale, for the trial had been an ordeal. Yet nothing had touched her beauty.

'I don't mind telling you,' said Reggie, 'that if it hadn't been for you, I think it would have been a dreadful business for Marion-Liz.' He'd caught the habit of the double name, and the girl answered to it naturally. 'It was a bright idea, you know, threatening Woolf that she'd ask you for help. Pity she didn't tell you the whole story, but—' He shrugged. 'You can understand it, can't you?'

Rollison just smiled.

The young man immediately sounded aggressive.

'Well? Can't you?'

'Oh, yes,' said Rollison brightly. 'Easily. By the way, Reggie, why did you come to Hilton Street?'

'Eh? Damn it, you're not going into that again! I gave my evidence, it was a place where I discovered Marion-Liz might have hidden. I just had to see her – can't you understand that, too? I'd give – my life to help her.'

The girl glanced at him, and knew that he meant it.

'No perjury?' murmured the Toff.

Rowse jumped up.

'Look here, that's an insult!'

'Not a deadly one,' said Rollison mildly. 'Nothing like the insults I've been saving up. Liz, look at me.'

She looked at him; she was just – lovely.

'I am now going to tell you the things you didn't tell

the police. First – about the missing buoy at the cove. You knew it was missing. Keller went out at dawn and unfastened it. You went down to swim, knowing I was watching. I behaved very nicely, but if I hadn't noticed the missing buoy, you were going to get into difficulties and I was going to save you. That would make me a hero.'

Rowse cried, 'You're crazy!'

'Everyone says so, but listen longer. Liz, you staged those quarrels with Eddie-Harry for my benefit. It was all done for my benefit. The story that Keller wanted to rob me, then you quarrelled, then you decided to have a go, was obviously phoney. Reggie came down to see you, and you quarrelled with him – just to impress me. His story stank to high heaven – the offered cigarettes and tobacco story was obviously made up. Remember? The quarrelling was thrust under my nose, even the manhandling by the yew-hedge in a spot I couldn't miss – Liz screamed to bring me to the window. So, said I, why? It was a put-up job, my lovebirds, and you put up a lot of it, Liz!'

Marion-Liz started violently, and said huskily, 'Yes?'

'You told me the truth about yourself, within limits, but you forgot to say that you had a third partner in the confidence tricks which you and Eddie-Harry had worked and planned to work. Our Reggie.'

Reggie clenched his fists. Marion-Liz stirred restlessly, and began to look less happy.

'And it was all beautifully worked out,' said Rollison dreamily. 'I was to help Reggie to reform you, Liz, and get myself completely tied up. I was to trust Reggie completely, and when you'd reached that stage – *abracadabra*. All the time, an old friend of mine, named sceptic, kept me company when I was with you. He was wise. What's behind it, Liz?'

She didn't answer.

Reginald Rowse just stood with his hands clenched.

'Tell me, how were you going to work the trick?' asked Rollison. 'What did you hope to get out of me?'

No one spoke; but there was guilt in two pairs of eyes. Rollison chuckled.

'Let's leave that for a minute. All went well, up to a point. Then Eddie-Harry came back to tell you that Woolf was on the war-path again. Woolf sent a message, purporting to come from Harry, summoning you to Hexley, but had the other girl handy in case you didn't go. Why didn't you try to go? I'd have driven you.'

Marion-Liz answered almost inaudibly, 'I thought it was a trick. Woolf's trick.'

'And were you right! Woolf planned his game perfectly, and Eddie-Harry died. Then you had to forget about your little plot with me, and worry about the really serious business. Right, Marion-Liz?'

'It – yes. Yes, it's true.'

'Why such an elaborate plan to win my confidence?' asked Rollison mildly.

Rowse said, 'What – what are you going to do?'

'Let's handle it stage by stage, Reggie. Why were you so anxious to get me in the web?'

Marion-Liz said hoarsely, 'I almost hate myself. I hoped you'd never know.'

'Don't hate yourself, tell me the truth.'

'All right,' she said, and Rowse groaned. 'You're quite right. We wanted your help. We thought it would work that way. It was Harry Keller's idea. You see – we know who can tell us where to find the Riordon Collection, and where to find the keys needed. We don't know where it is, but – my father does. Yes, my father's in gaol, I know. I've told you how I feel about him. We couldn't get at him, but you were friendly with the police. We were going to tell you everything, and suggest that if you could get the Riordon Collection, it would be a great triumph for the Toff. We were sure you'd fall for it – you'd manage to see Father, give him a message from me, find out where the Collection was.'

Rowse said, 'Oh, hell! We were all going to find it together, Rollison, and we'd have some strong-arm boys on the spot. We'd have dealt with you, just knocked you cold, and got off with the stuff.'

'Have another drink,' said Rollison hospitably.

'What are you going to do?' muttered Rowse.

'Do? Just what you planned, with a minor exception – get the truth out of your father, Liz, and pass it on to the police. Simple.'

'But – us?'

'You? I'm going to be a witness at your wedding, and I'm going to be a benevolent uncle, keeping an eye on you for a long time. Until you've given up the crazy idea of avenging yourself on an innocent society.'

Marion-Liz was crying silently.

Reginald Rowse looked like a schoolboy caught out in a heinous crime.

The front-door bell rang.

Lady Gloria and Iris arrived together and appeared to notice nothing remarkable about the puffy redness at Marion-Liz's eyes.

*   *   *

Rollison and Grice stood in the passage, beneath a house near Watford, a house owned by Marion-Liz's father and let to tenants who had no idea what was below their cellar. Grice held a set of keys in his hand.

He handed them to Rollison.

'Bill,' said Rollison, as he turned the key, 'did I ever say I was sorry I clouted you?'

'No.'

'Well, I am. You will for ever be my favourite police-man.'

He pushed at the heavy door.

Torches flashed about a dark vault, cobwebs hung down on packing-cases and boxes and safes. Grice's men came in and were busy with crowbars and keys. More light was brought in and shone on jewels which brought fire into the vaults; on *objets d'art* and oil-paintings; on a fortune.